Journey to Die For

Radine Trees Nehring

Wolfmont Press

This novel is a work of fiction. Names, characters, places and
incidents are either the product of the author's imaginations or are
used fictitiously, and any resemblance to actual persons, living or
dead, business establishments, events or locales is entirely
coincidental, except as noted.

JOURNEY TO DIE FOR

ISBN: 978-1-60364-020-6

Edited by Tony Burton
Cover art by Cat Rahmeier

www.radinesbooks.com
Printed in the United States of America

Published by Wolfmont Press
A division of Wolfmont LLC
238 Park Drive NE — Ranger, GA 30734
editor@wolfmont.com — www.wolfmont.com

Library of Congress Control Number: 2010927784
Publisher's Cataloging-In-Publication

Nehring, Radine Trees, 1935-
Journey to die for / Radine Trees Nehring.--1st ed.
    p. cm.
    ISBN: 978-1-60364-020-6

    1. McCrite, Carrie (Fictitious character)—Fiction. 2. Ozark
Mountains—Fiction. 3. Van Buren (Ark.)—Fiction. 4.
Arkansas and Missouri Railroad—Fiction. 5. Trains—
Arkansas—Fiction. 6. Older women—Fiction. I. Title.

PS3614.E44J68 2010
813'.6—dc22
2010927784

To my "more than a sister"

Catherine Rahmeier

Acknowledgments

Many people in many locations were my guides during the writing of this story.

To begin at the beginning: Thanks to Brenda Brown, Passenger Train Operations Manager for the Arkansas and Missouri Railroad, to Stephanie Demetre, her assistant, and the rest of the A&M office staff. Thanks also to A&M conductors Russell and Charlene Kelly.

Special thanks to Arkansas Educational Television Network star Chuck Dovish for his weekly program, "Exploring Arkansas, and the segment that featured the A&M excursion trip to Van Buren. I also appreciate the added information Chuck shared about filming the A&M day trip.

Thanks to Holly Houser Cherry, Historical Park Interpreter at Prairie Grove Battlefield State Park in Arkansas, who helped with some of the Civil War information I share in these pages.

In Van Buren, many thanks to Cami Brown, Planning Assistant for the City of Van Buren, to Nadean Riley Bell, who knows Van Buren's stories, and Larry Brandenburg, Bookseller, who welcomed me, helped me find history books, and explained houseboat living on the Arkansas River. Larry is the one who found **The Civil War Diary of Private Henry A. Strong, Co. K, Twelfth Kansas Infantry**, edited by Tom Wing, for me. (Private Strong spent a lot of his time in the military in and around Van Buren. If you want inside information about the Civil War, read a soldier's diary!)

In the Van Buren Police Department, thanks to CID secretary Sandra Carney, and Administrative secretary Melissa Wright; to Lt. Brent Grill, Desk Sgt. Jim Hurst, Detective Rick Patterson, and Communications Officer Steve Pitchford. You were all patient and helpful in responding to my questions. (Parts of this work of fiction deviate from truth on the ground in the VBPD. Y'all pardon me for taking liberties. And no, I've never tasted your coffee. However, I have tasted the food at Carol's Cafe in Van Buren and it's just as good as characters in this novel say it is.)

Other very helpful law enforcement information was provided by Police Chief Trent Morrison and Sgt. John Dunham in the Gravette, AR Police Department, as well as (over the years) several police officers in Kansas City, and Doris Jackson, paralegal in the Legal Department of the KCPD.

Any mistakes about police department functions are mine, not those of the people I interviewed.

And thanks to career police officer and author Lee Lofland, whose blog account of "The Day I Killed the Bank Robber" helped me learn what killing a crazed convenience store robber had been like for Henry King.

Finally, my heartfelt gratitude to my husband John, who helps and supports my work in uncountable ways; to gifted cover artist Cat Rahmeier; and to Tony Burton, editor and friend supreme.

"BOARD! ALL ABOARD"

The woman had been talking forever.

Carrie looked at her watch and discovered "forever" was only about fifteen minutes, but in that time she'd heard more about the woman and her husband than any stranger ought to know. She also knew the couple had come to Arkansas on vacation mainly to ride the historic excursion train from Springdale to Van Buren. "We collect rides on real trains," the woman explained.

"Umhmm," Carrie said. She was alone in her boredom. Henry had deserted her several minutes earlier, saying he wanted to watch the train's engineer line up the cars to be used today. Claude, the woman's husband, had left long ago to do the same thing.

The woman took a breath and said, "Well, now. How about you? Are you and your husband retired? You look old enough to be retired. Claude and I are way too young to retire, but we'll probably be unlocking the door of our business as long as we can toddle there. So, what did you retire from?"

Carrie, suddenly feeling very wicked, said, "Oh, we're not retired. We're private detectives."

"My, how, uh, very unique. I guess you chase after people who owe money, spy on wayward husbands, stuff like that. I know if Claude ever—"

"No," Carrie interrupted, "we chase after murderers." Then she walked away, hoping Henry never found out what she'd just said.

"Board! All aboard," the conductor called.

1

When their turn to board came, Henry climbed up first and extended a hand down to her. The conductor hovered, waiting to give a judicious boost if such were required. "Golly these steps are high," Carrie said. "They're like I remember from when I rode the train home for college vacations all those years ago. You'd think by now...." She grasped Henry's hand and swung up. The momentum rocketed her against him with a *whump*, and his free arm went around her.

"Well, my dear, I think the reason these steps are as high as you remember is because this railway coach was built in the 1920's, quite a few years before you went to college."

"Oh, well, um, yes. For goodness' sake, let's move on. People are waiting in line."

He released her and they went through the vestibule into the coach. "Where do you want to sit?" he asked.

"Near the back. We'll have more window space in front of us."

"Good. You take the window seat. I can see over your head."

Carrie dropped onto a green velvet double seat three rows from the back of the coach, then put her tote bag on the floor under her seat so Henry would have plenty of room.

After a moment of silence she looked up at him. "My love, this is a great anniversary present. I've wanted to take this day-trip to Van Buren for ages, but never got around to it. I do feel a bit guilty though, since Eleanor, Jason, Shirley, and Roger have talked about wanting to make the trip too. Maybe we should have done it together."

"Nope," Henry said, "we're celebrating eight months of marriage on our own. Besides, the anniversary train ride was Eleanor's idea in the first place."

Carrie grinned, said, "I must thank her," and then turned to look out the window. "I wonder how long before we leave."

"Don't know. The flyer said departure was eight o'clock, but there are still quite a few people out there waiting to board."

"Henry, look, *look!*" Her finger jabbed the window." Isn't that Chuck Dovish, the guy we watch on TV?"

"Umm?"

"You know, the one who does the 'Exploring Arkansas' program on Public Television. That's gotta be him, black hair, mustache, and all. See? Over there, standing on the platform, talking to a man with a video camera." She bounced in her seat. "Henry, I think we're going to be on TV."

STRANGERS ON A TRAIN

"I knew there had to be something good about getting up before dawn," Carrie said. "We sure got good seats."

"Yes. But you know, trains show you the backsides of towns, people's back yards and garbage cans and the places where everyone–businesses and homeowners–stack all the junk they think they might use some day and never do."

"Oh, I know, Henry, but the flyer calls this a scenic tour, so I imagine we'll see plenty of good stuff too. It says we ride through the Boston Mountains, cross several tall trestles, and go through the highest railway tunnel between the Appalachians and the Rockies. I looked at a map. We travel alongside a river for a while, and go right through Frog Bayou. Therefore, I will not be turned off by your talk of garbage cans." She crossed her arms over her chest and tried not to laugh.

Henry laughed instead. "It was just a warning. Didn't want you to be disappointed."

"I promise I'll enjoy it all, even the garbage cans. It's the train ride itself, and seeing the historic district of Van Buren, that I'm looking forward to."

She watched a woman shepherding two children, about four and six, toward the train steps, then gasped as a man dressed in khaki slacks and a black polo shirt shoved ahead of them to board. The tote he carried whacked one of the children on the arm, but he seemed not to notice. The little girl stared up at him and rubbed her arm, but, thank goodness, she didn't cry. The mother, however, looked angry enough to spit nails.

"Henry, I saw—"

"Look there, Cara. Maybe we really are going to be on television. Chuck Dovish just came into this car. He's sitting up front. I don't see a cameraman, but I suppose he could still be outside, filming the engine and cars and other outside stuff."

"Henry King, did you plan this as a special surprise? Did you know about it?"

"Can't take credit, Little Love; there's no way I could have known. And, right now I'm more interested in seeing how they actually do filming for television than I am in being part of the program. I can compare what I see here with what we eventually see on TV."

She nodded. "We'll certainly have something to tell everyone when we get back home this evening."

They fell silent as they watched the last of the passengers board the train and Carrie's thoughts were occupied with remembering snippets from some of the "Exploring Arkansas" programs they had watched. Chuck Dovish climbing a sheer rock wall and leaping around in triumph when he made it to the top. Chuck Dovish crawling through numerous Arkansas caves with varying features, and usually emerging mud-soaked. Chuck Dovish attending a hot air balloon event near Bentonville. Chuck Dovish canoeing on the Buffalo National River, Chuck Dovish....

The woman and her two children came in the car and settled on a seat across the aisle from Dovish. The man in the black shirt hurried down the aisle and sat in front of Henry, joining a man wearing a blue shirt who had already taken the window seat. Both bobbed heads in a brief greeting, but otherwise ignored each other.

The platform finally emptied. The last one to board was the cameraman, but he wasn't filming when the television host stood and moved into the aisle. He introduced himself and the cameraman, said they were from AETN, then went on, "If anyone here is uncomfortable about being filmed and possibly appearing on an 'Exploring Arkansas' program, you might want to move into the car behind this one. The conductor assures me you'll find plenty of good seats there. We'll be filming scenery and talking with the conductor, but we'll also use this car to show people enjoying the ride. I'll talk with some of you about what you think of the experience. Everyone okay with that?"

Carrie could see nodding heads all along the car, but right in front of her, Blue Shirt's head jerked, and he started to get up. Then, body still bent, he stopped moving as if struck with paralysis. In a moment he sat again and turned to stare out the window. At the same time Black Shirt had leaned out into the aisle, looking toward the opening into the car behind them. Then he too hesitated, turned a quick glance toward his seat companion's back, and settled in his seat, staring straight ahead.

Odd.

Did those guys know each other? Carrie studied what she could see of them. All she could tell about the man in the blue shirt was that his shirt was oxford cloth and he was blond. He looked the younger of the two. You never knew about pale blonds, though. Maybe his washed-out hair color concealed some grey.

Dovish began talking again. "If you're all okay with our plans, I guess I can say, 'Welcome to Exploring Arkansas,' because that's really what this trip is about for all of us, isn't it?"

As the train jerked and began moving, he grabbed the edge of his seat back. "It feels like we're on our way. Now, I need your help with something. At all times, will you please ignore the cameraman? During some of the ride he'll be taking general shots in the car and of the scenery outside. Try and pretend he isn't here." He grinned, and looked over at his companion. "He's a pretty big guy, but do the best you can to imagine he's invisible. And thanks for your part in helping us show people all over Arkansas and in neighboring states what a ride on this historic train is like."

He stopped talking as the train whistle sounded two long blasts, and then repeated itself in a short hoot and another long blast. He lifted his hands and shoulders in a gesture of helplessness and waited until the sound died. "Did you know that two long, one short, and another long whistle like we just heard is the warning signal for a crossing? You'll hear it a lot during this trip." He grinned at them again and sat down.

"He smiles just like you see on TV," Carrie said.

"Not too surprising," Henry replied absently as he turned in his seat to look around the car. "This coach is sure fancy. I'd bet the paneling is mahogany. Those are real stained glass windows all along the top, and just look at the ceiling fans. I wonder if many passenger rail cars from the 1920's were this elegant. The Arkansas and Missouri Railroad folks must have done quite a bit of restoration work in here."

"Probably did," Carrie said, "but look outside now. There are your back yards, junk, and garbage cans. No wonder the guy with the camera is filming inside. TV viewers might be turned off by pictures of garbage cans."

As the photographer moved slowly down the aisle, she poked at Henry, who was still studying the car's interior. "Is my hair okay?"

"Yes, it's fine."

"You didn't even look at me."

He turned toward her and smiled. "It was fine a minute ago. It's always fine, and you know it. Your naturally curly hair stays the same. It doesn't even look messy when you get up in the morning. It's not messy now."

She sighed, reached down for her tote, and took out a small mirror to survey her grey curls. Well, Henry was right, it was fine. Except for haircuts, washing, and occasional combing, she never needed to fuss with her hair.

As she put the mirror away she noticed that Black Shirt now had a ball cap pulled low on his forehead. It looked like he was reading something lying in his lap. Blue Shirt was reading the railway's information flyer, unfolded all the way and held in front of his face as if he were shortsighted. Both men had slid down in their seats and seemed to be sitting on their spines.

Why?

A CURIOUS WOMAN

What was it with those guys? Carrie's curiosity—
what Henry called her "seventh sense"—was coming on
strong. Something about the two men looked... well, it
just looked fishy. She wondered if Henry had noticed
anything, but since the men were so close she didn't dare
talk to him about it. He'd say it wasn't her business
anyway. Strictly speaking, that was right. But one
couldn't help observing things and, after all, you never
knew when odd bits of observation might become
important.

Too bad she wasn't taller. Too bad the seat backs
were solid. Too bad the men weren't sitting across the
aisle from them so she could cast a judicious glance their
way every so often.

Might at least one of them be engaged in some
criminal activity? Or could they both be law officers,
working under cover? Why didn't either man, two
strangers it seemed, want to be filmed for television?
Coincidence?

She could get a better look if she walked to the front
of the car to use the toilet. But that offered only a short,
one-time view, and traipsing back and forth in the aisle
too frequently would be embarrassing. The train ride was
so smooth she couldn't claim motion sickness. Which
reminded her....

"Henry, I don't feel the rhythmic *click-clack* trains
are supposed to make. What's wrong?"

"Nothing's wrong. These days rails are welded

smoothly. Few bumpy joints."

"I miss it."

"Well, I guess I do, too." He took her hand, squeezed it, and they grinned at each other. *We're like goofy teenagers,* Carrie thought, and wondered what the people sitting behind them made of their actions.

He asked, "Were you looking out your window when we passed the horse farm, or were you too involved with... something else?" He pointed a finger at the back of the seat in front of them.

"I, uhhh...."

"Thought so. You missed quite a spread. Looked like miles of white fence surrounding green pastures. Lots of horses. There's big money tied up in that operation."

"Plenty of big money in Benton County. Wal-Mart headquarters, you know."

"Except we're in Washington County now. We passed the University of Arkansas in Fayetteville several minutes ago."

"Money is allowed to move over county lines."

He laughed. "Right."

For a while she watched tumbling river water when it appeared beside the tracks, then turned her head slightly to check on the two men. Neither of them had looked out the window until after the photographer went to the front of the car to film Dovish's conversation with the conductor.

Something about those guys was just plain peculiar.

* * *

Henry shut his eyes for a moment. She was at it

again. His sweet wife was puzzling about the behavior of the men sitting in front of them, and what the dickens could he do about it?

He'd cautioned her repeatedly about problems that might come from too much interest in other folk's business, but it looked like she'd never change. Her strong interest in people sometimes turned her into– what would he call it? A snoop? A busybody? No, those sounded brutal. Maybe he should think of her as... as... an instinctive detective.

She'd undoubtedly noticed how negatively both men acted toward being photographed, though they obviously didn't want to be seen as avoiding the camera. Trouble was, he sensed something wrong about those guys too, so how could he blame her for a heightened interest?

If only it didn't go any further than that.

If only she was better at tempering curiosity with wisdom.

Ignore them. Stay out of it, let's just enjoy our special day together, he wanted to say, but couldn't because they might hear him. Hey, wait. He could write her a note.

Henry felt in his pockets. No paper.

He knew well enough she'd react negatively to being warned off any interest in those two anyway, even if he could speak to her about it now. She'd simply point to his own interest in people, not to mention his tendency to imagine pending criminal activity where there was none.

Usually was none.

He opened his eyes and stared over her head into

distant hills. He wished he could erase a few leftover memories from his long years in the Kansas City Police Department. It was okay to have a friendly interest in people, but a unique talent for noticing suspicious activity was definitely not a plus in his life today, nor was his heart-stopping fear for Carrie's safety when she got involved with potentially bad people. Knowing the awful things some humans could do to each other was a legacy from police work. He'd seen, first hand, the horrible endings, the brutality, the....

Stop it!

Carrie said his former profession gave him an educated insight into people's needs, and that was a good thing.

Well, maybe. Most of the time it seemed like a curse, not something to be welcomed.

True, his insight had helped save Carrie's life once when she was in danger through no fault of her own. Other times—well, she was sometimes better at getting into messes than out of them.

No, that wasn't fair. She'd saved him from a hellish mess in Hot Springs, when he'd been the one who was curious about Everett Bogardus's actions in the first place.

Trouble was, he hadn't been able to sort all this out yet. It was hardly the thing ordinary couples in love were expected to come to terms with.

"Henry, when we're in a unique position to help people, we should do it. That's a blessing, not a curse."

He started to say "Maybe you're right," aloud, but

then realized he'd only imagined she was repeating words she'd said to him months ago.

He frowned. Should they have turned away from helping people when they clearly could? Sure, sometimes it had been family or friends, like when JoAnne was murdered, or when his sister Catherine and Carrie's son Rob got into trouble at Buffalo National River. That was different. But other times the people had been strangers. So, what about the strangers?

What about now?

Ahh, but now was off the table. No one needed help here and, no matter how strange the two guys acted, they had nothing to do with Carrie McCrite or Henry King.

"Winslow tunnel, coming up," the conductor said. "1700 feet long. The grade has been so gradual, I'll bet few of you realized how much we were climbing. Winslow is the highest incorporated town in Arkansas."

Henry reached over and put his arm around Carrie. When they reached the tunnel, he'd hug her tight all the way through.

JOURNEY INTO HISTORY

"It's a-l-l-l down hill from now on," the conductor said as they left the total darkness of the tunnel. He paused, shaking his head while surveying his passenger's faces.

"Well, what on earth does he mean?" Carrie asked, as she and Henry pulled apart like teenagers caught making out. "All down hill?"

Henry didn't answer, but he was grinning as the conductor continued. "What I'm saying, of course, is that we're beginning our descent into the Arkansas River Valley. Oh, did you not know that's what *down* hill means?"

Carrie chuckled, along with almost everyone else in the car.

"The Arkansas River has always been important to Van Buren. It offered shipping access to the Mississippi and the world beyond long before there were railroads in the area.

"A man named Thomas Phillips established Phillips' Landing near the river's major curve in 1818. In the 1830's the town's name was changed to Van Buren, after then Secretary of State Martin Van Buren, who became the eighth president of the United States in 1837, as I am sure all of you remember."

He winked at them and went on. "By the time Van Buren took the oath of office, two sharp businessmen named John Drennen and David Thompson had bought the town from Phillips for a reported eleven thousand dollars. They established a business selling firewood to flat-bottom steamboats plying the river, and also advertised the area's amenities in southern newspapers. 'Payment for lots,' their ad said, 'is accepted in Mississippi, Tennessee, Alabama, Louisiana, or other bank notes.'"

"Did states print their own money?" Carrie asked.

"Sounds like it," Henry said.

The conductor continued. "Since overland freight shipments were all propelled by horses, mules, or oxen back then, the presence of a river that was navigable, at least some of the time, was important for commerce. I'm thinking Drennen and Thompson must have raked in the money as Van Buren developed into a thriving river port.

"It wasn't all smooth steaming, however. There are a lot of boats at the bottom of the Arkansas River. In fact, during much of the 1800's, the Arkansas demanded the second highest insurance rates of any American river. It was surpassed only by the Red River. Water in both rivers could easily be too low for safe travel, and many boats ran aground or hit snags. In addition, Confederate boats were burned and sunk near Van Buren during the Civil War, helping give the river one of its nick-names, 'Steamboat Graveyard.'

"Which brings us to railroads. And, speaking of that, on the left you'll see the town of Chester, which used to be a rail hub on this line, with a roundhouse and busy rail yards. The two-story brick building on the corner was once a railroad hotel, now an antique shop; it's said to be haunted."

The conductor returned to his seat as everyone, including the two men in front of Carrie and Henry, looked toward Chester's haunted hotel.

Carrie's attention popped back into the car when Chuck Dovish stood. Golly, she'd better get busy thinking up things to say about this trip. She could tell him it was an anniversary gift from her husband. That ought to make it into the TV program.

But Dovish didn't come their way. He only moved across the aisle as he and the man with the camera turned their attention to the mother with two small children. Well, they were cute kids, and the little girl had already begun talking excitedly in response to some question or other.

Rob wouldn't have done that. Her son would probably have tucked his face against her side and remained silent. He still had a problem with conversation—unless he was lecturing to one of his anthropology or American Indian history classes at the university. *Professor* Rob McCrite never ran out of words. Ah, well. Maybe Catherine could teach him the art of social conversation. Dating Henry's much younger and very talkative half-sister had already enhanced Rob's ability to interact with humans who weren't in an academic setting.

Carrie went back to watching scenery and glancing—only occasionally—toward the seat in front of her. The two men were now behaving like ordinary passengers. She saw them exchange brief comments now and then, which would be normal for strangers who had no particular interest in each other.

She surprised herself by being glad about that. After all, this was a fun trip planned by Henry as a special gift to her. She had no reason to be concerned about those men. It was time to stop speculating about them and spend every bit of time enjoying this day.

Watching scenery slide past had begun to make her fell drowsy when Dovish returned to his seat and the conductor stood to continue his history lesson.

"In 1882 this rail line was completed, linking Van Buren to St. Louis and beyond, and making the town an important rail junction. The Frisco Passenger Depot we'll be seeing at our destination was completed in 1901 and is still in use as a depot and museum.

"Passenger travel dwindled toward the middle of the last century, and was discontinued in 1965, though the line continued to carry freight. Then, twenty or so years ago, the Arkansas and Missouri Railroad folks decided they'd like to re-open limited passenger service for tourists and anyone else who wanted to experience rail travel as it was in the 'good old days.' They began a search for historic cars that hadn't been dismantled for scrap, and ended up with four. Those cars were restored, and this excursion train ran for the first time in 1992. The cars you're riding in today initially saw service some time between 1917 and the early 1930's. A&M found and added L'il Toot, our antique caboose, in 2006."

He took out a big pocket watch, studied its face, and then held it up for all to see. "My father was a railroad man, and this was his watch. It still keeps perfect time, and tells me now that our estimated time of arrival in Van Buren is 10:40.

"There will be a short pause after we enter town while the engine switches to the opposite end of the train and pushes us into the station. Please stay in your seats, since we'll experience a few bumps and jerks. I'll let you know when it's time to get off.

"You'll have three hours to enjoy your tour of Van Buren's historic district. In addition to many shops, there are several good restaurants along Main Street to serve you when you get hungry.

"Be back at the station by two o'clock, ready to board for the return trip. Mr. Dovish from AETN will be with us again on the ride back, and he plans to chat with a few more of you about your impressions of today's journey into history.

"Remember now, we'll be boarding at two. I'll see all of you back here then."

Carrie touched Henry's arm. "I'm eager to be off the train so we can begin exploring antique shops."

"Oh. Were you planning to buy something?"

"Who knows? Eleanor and Jason have driven down here more than once to go antiquing. She told me Jason likes to look at the old tools and toys in a shop called Fletcher's, so we need to find that place. Many of the shops sell fancier stuff, though. You know, china, glass, and jewelry. She says there's furniture, too."

"Carrie, I hope you aren't thinking of doing much shopping, especially for furniture. I didn't see a freight car on this train."

She frowned. "Well, no, but for gosh' sake Henry, we could drive back to pick up something if it was too big to carry."

He pursed his lips and said nothing, then turned away to watch the engine move past windows on the other side of their car as it began a switch to the opposite end of the train.

Uh-oh. Carrie wondered what he'd thought they were going to do for the three hours they'd be in Van Buren. Sit on a bench and people-watch? Of course they'd go shopping; that's what everyone came to do. She felt just a tiny tinge of impatience, and then, sadness. Actually, other than groceries and the time he went with her to select Christmas gifts, she and Henry hadn't shopped as a couple since their marriage. But, she'd never thought...well, wouldn't they enjoy looking at things together? And, after all, she was the one with money. She could jolly well spend it however she wanted.

Thinking that stopped her cold. If she ever said aloud to Henry what she'd just thought, well, it might be hurtful. And how could she even *think* it?

Sure, he knew she had her former husband's money now, and that it amounted to a lot more than his own police pension, but they'd never, ever talked about it. For eight months she'd been so careful not to make anything of who paid what bills.

When they first met, she was the one who needed a paying job to help make ends meet; she was the one who had less money. It hadn't mattered who had what back then. Why should it matter now?

Well, Carrie, who says it does matter?

Maybe this was only a problem inside her head. Henry had never said anything, or acted like his male ego was being crushed because he had a wife with money. At that, Carrie almost laughed aloud. Which wife? His first wife had been very wealthy. He must be used to women with money by now. At that she sighed, forgetting that he would hear her.

"What's the matter, Little Love?"

"Oh, well, I was just thinking."

"A penny."

Must he? What could she possibly say?

"Well, I'm just sorry you don't want to go shopping."

"I...."

A bump. The train began moving again, oh so slowly, and Henry's words matched its speed. "I've never gone antique shopping. Irena sure did, though. She was constantly adding more stuff to the house. Cut glass and china and porcelain figures and silver. All kinds of fancy junk. It was her money, and she paid the maids who dusted and polished all of it, so why should I care what she bought? I just had to be careful I didn't break anything.

"Carrie, all I know about shopping is buying socks and underwear and shirts. Of course, after the divorce I had to shop for food and basic household necessities, but that wasn't much. I ate out most of the time."

She spoke hesitantly. "We go grocery shopping together. That's shopping."

He stared at her as if some great enlightenment had

dawned on him. "Going grocery shopping with you is entertainment. You see more possibilities than I ever did. We talk about what we want, look at new ways food is presented, even laugh at a few of them. Much better than rushing in to grab the few items I had to have when I lived alone."

"Van Buren," the conductor called out. "Van Buren, Arkansas. Please stay in your seats until the train is fully stopped, and check to be sure you have all your possessions with you. Don't leave anything in the car. We'll see you all back here in three hours."

"Y'know," Henry said, "I'm hungry. Breakfast was gosh-awful early. Let's look for a place to eat."

She grinned, reached for his hand, and gave it a squeeze. "Sounds good to me. We'll go shopping for lunch."

A DAY TO DIE FOR

"Talk about the good old days," Henry said, scraping a fork across his empty plate and then licking the tines. "I haven't seen the words 'plate lunch' on a restaurant window in years, nor have I eaten real peeled-on-site mashed potatoes in any restaurant lately. I swear, Carrie, I'd almost drive all the way here to eat Carol's chicken-fried steak again."

"I agree, it was delicious," Carrie said, looking past him out the window. "So why don't you have some of that pie with ice cream while I look in a few shops?"

"Well, if you wouldn't mind.... How about meeting me back here in half an hour or so? If I finish and they get crowded, I'll wait on the bench outside."

"Okay. See you later."

Carrie managed a quick look through one shop with stock that was more collectable than antique, then moved slowly through the next one, enjoying the cut crystal serving pieces displayed there. She finally selected a deeply cut English crystal nappy that would be perfect for dressing up store-bought preserves. Making conversation while the shop owner was wrapping it, she admitted she'd like to know more about Van Buren's history.

"Came in on the train, you say? Well, you haven't much time, then. If you're on the Internet they have history, and stories about many of our Main Street buildings. Just Google 'Van Buren, Arkansas.' And you might try Brandenburg Books across from the depot. It's mostly used books, and Larry sometimes finds gems of local history.

"You know, though, the fastest way you'll learn our history is to look at the painted mural wall in Riverfront Park. It was done by local art students about thirty years ago, and tells the town's story in logical sequence. Kind of a short course, but a good overall idea of our rich heritage."

"That sounds perfect. How do we get there? Is it far?"

The woman handed Carrie her package, then looked at her doubtfully. "How are you for walking?" It's several blocks to the river, but the walk goes pretty fast unless you stop off in shops along the way. It's at the end of Main Street, and getting there is all downhill, but coming back is a pretty tough chug, even for youngsters."

"Ah. Well, I walk at home, but hill climbing slows me down quite a bit. Maybe we can drive back here this fall to see it."

Carrie's disappointment must have shown, because, after a thoughtful pause, the woman said, "I live in a houseboat beside the park, and I'm going home for lunch as soon as Iris comes to relieve me. If you walk down there, I'll drive you back." She looked at her watch. "I could meet you by the park's entrance at, say, one o'clock?"

"My husband is with me. I left him eating pie at Carol's."

The woman laughed. "And no wonder. But don't you worry, there's room for both of you in my car, even if he's swelled up with Carol's cooking. You go on and get him now, and I'll see you at the park gate about one. I'll be in a red Toyota."

"That's awfully kind, but I hate to bother you."

"No bother. I've got to drive back from the river anyway."

"Well then, we'll do it, and I thank you. Before I leave, though, I think I'll get that crystal pitcher I was admiring, and the gold pendant with the greenish stone in this case." She pointed. "It's next to the divider. Yes, that's it."

"Oh, I love that, too. The stone is kind of blue-green. It matches your eyes."

"That's what my husband will say." Carrie smiled up at her. "Will it be okay if I leave my packages here until we return?"

"Of course," the woman said.

It was easy to walk to the river without distractions because Henry barely glanced in shop windows and Carrie, wanting to have plenty of time in the park, didn't dally either. They took a moment to admire one of the oldest buildings in the area, the Crawford County Courthouse, but otherwise followed Main Street past shops, a small industrial section, and then through brick pillars into the park.

"My word, I had no idea the mural was this big," Carrie said as they turned left and stared at a wall full of color. They followed the wall, walking along the river next to a gated dock sheltering several large cabin cruisers. "And just look at the river. It must be a mile wide here. Seems as big as the Mississippi at St. Louis."

"Well, I think not quite that big," Henry said, "and don't forget there are locks and dams below here to enhance river travel. It is quite a distance to the other side, though. Maybe it looks wider because we're right on the bank at the river's level."

"Maybe. Now, where is the beginning of the mural? We seem to be at the end of the history it records."

"Look behind you. It must be down there, upriver."

"Oh, yes." She drew in a breath. "Gosh, it extends a couple of blocks, and I want to see the history in sequence." Assuming Henry would be right behind her she said nothing more and began walking rapidly along the road.

* * *

Henry wasn't aware Carrie had walked off. He'd been watching a man about his own age maneuver an impressive cabin cruiser away from the dock, and the purr of the engine was all he could hear.

He'd like to be on that boat. Sweet! Wouldn't it be great to have a craft like it, to cruise for miles along the river, thinking almost nothing, just watching the shore pass by? He'd let the splash and rock of river travel soothe him. *Sweet, sweet.*

The boat turned down river, catching the current. Henry wondered where the man was going. Maybe just for a pleasure ride.

He turned, "Carrie, did you see that...."

Where *was* Carrie? He looked around. Blast, she was almost out of sight. Time to forget boating and follow. But he would ask her if she was interested in large boats or had ever ridden in one. Maybe they would have more time to look at the boats here before the woman came to pick them up. Didn't Carrie say she lived in a houseboat? What would that be like? Probably like a motor home, except it would rock with the movement of the river.

* * *

She gazed at the colorful wall as she walked but–aware she was seeing history in reverse–hurried up river toward the first panel. When she found it she looked at her watch, and decided she had time to walk a bit farther, maybe to the base of the railroad bridge. She liked being this close to the river and, for a moment, wondered if it there were boats for rent anywhere around here. Maybe she and Henry could rent a boat and take a ride on the river this fall. She'd have to ask him if he knew how to drive anything bigger than a fishing boat.

She glanced back and saw him in the distance. Good. He could see her and wouldn't worry about where she'd gone.

The railroad bridge looked old, its oval pillars of concrete and stone stained and blackened. A thicket of brush and trees clustered in the water near the bridge. An island? Maybe. The river was still high from unusually heavy spring rains, so those trees could be part of the normal shoreline. She found a path and walked toward the water, lamenting that trash had accumulated along its edge. Some of the trash had washed up onto the shore. The water was quite shallow here; shallow enough that a large clump of cloth soaked in mud had caught in the weedy growth next to the bank.

She blinked, blinked again, shut her eyes.

No! It could not be; it just couldn't. She opened her eyes and turned away from the river. The image was an illusion, born of past experiences and an over-active imagination. Those two men... Henry was right. She should have ignored them.

She stared into the brushy tangle on the opposite side of the road, wishing the image away. Forget the seventh sense, forget the times she'd told Henry they'd been given opportunities to help people in trouble simply because they could. This was a stupid illusion and it wouldn't be there when she looked back. *She had seen nothing.*

If she started walking toward Henry no one would know what she might have seen.

Then Carrie turned toward the river again because she had to.

Blue shirt. Pale blond hair. Face down in the mud-heavy water. She couldn't see the face, but what did that matter? She hadn't been able to see the face of the man sitting in front of her on the train either.

Could he be alive? The water moved. Ripples splashed. Was he moving too, or was it her imagination? She took two steps toward him, intending to get close enough to check for a pulse and at least get his head out of the water.

Instinctively she looked at the ground and saw a large footprint in the mud. Whose?

Two more steps now. *Look carefully, Carrie, keep looking at the ground. Do not disturb anything. This may be... may be... a crime scene. Is that grass disturbed because the man was dragged here, or could the splash and pull of a boat wake cause it to bend over like that? But, wouldn't the clump of trees out there stop any wake?*

She stooped and reached out, not noticing that her walking shoes were sinking into the soggy bank. She found an arm, slippery with mud, felt the wrist, couldn't detect even a faint flutter. Her hand was still in the water when Henry appeared beside her, silent and strong. He pulled her gently away from the river's edge, then picked up a take-out pizza carton that had washed onto the grass near them. When he lifted the man's head they both saw the clouded, staring eyes. "He's gone," was all he said.

Henry laid the head on the carton and pulled out his cell phone.

MAN ON A RIVER BANK

"The police are coming. We'll wait here."

"Of course," she said as he reached out, sheltering her in his arms.

"Are you okay?"

"Yes."

He held her another moment, then kissed the top of her head before moving away to scan the riverbank.

She watched him, aware of the exact second when years of police experience and training took charge of her dear, gentle husband.

"Is it the man from the train?" she asked, trying hard to sound professional.

"Possibly. Blue shirt, blond hair, but I never got a look at that man's face."

The former law officer was speaking now, cautious, unwilling to make definite statements. "It looks like he drowned. Autopsy will tell. I guess he could have fallen in—from a boat, maybe, but why would he be out on the river now, when the train's return trip is at 2:00?"

"Is suicide possible?" she asked. "I didn't see any wounds, but then I haven't looked at much of him, only his arm and head."

Water splashed against the shore a few inches below the grass, and the man's torso moved again as she stared at it. "Henry, are those cuts in his shirt? Knife cuts? What am I seeing?"

"Maybe knife cuts."

"I wish we could stop those waves. He's mostly

floating, and if any boat comes along, the wake could pull him back out in the river."

He lifted his head to search the river. "I don't see anything coming. I think larger boats and barges stay in a channel beyond the big island out there."

She shielded her eyes with her hand and looked too. "I wonder how long it's been since any boat came along this side. Might not hurt to know that."

"You're right. Could help set a time when this happened. But not long ago, I think."

She saw motion to their right and turned her head toward the road. "Jogger coming," she said.

They stood side-by-side, two tourists watching the river, while the runner went past behind them.

After he was out of sight, she glanced at Henry, who was studying the bank again. Would he be willing to tell the police that neither of them knew anything about this man except what they saw here? After all, it was basically true. They couldn't be sure it was the man from the train, could they? So why mention it? Then, when they'd answered a few questions, they could probably leave contact information and go about the rest of their day as planned.

But she knew Henry wouldn't agree to that, and, besides, she'd be a traitor to her own words about helping people whenever the two of them clearly could. That's what their forays into detecting had really been about.

She looked at the man on the river bank again. Actually, he was beyond their help, so they didn't need to become involved here.

No. That was wrong. Truth and justice made a difference. Carrie sighed. This was a nightmare. They might not even be allowed to return on the train–but then, how would they get home?

Henry's voice broke into her thoughts. She recognized his flat tones from other times when they'd faced disasters like this together. "Did you notice how the body felt when you touched the arm?"

She winced at his impersonal reference to the man lying dead below them, but answered professionally as she knew he expected her to. "Pliable. But we've only been in Van Buren a little over..." she looked at her watch. "Oh! It's one o'clock. We're supposed to be back on the train in an hour, and that lady from the antiques shop is waiting to pick us up at the park gate right now. Couldn't we tell the police an absolute minimum and get away from here more quickly?"

"We'll do the best we can, but you know it's got to be the right thing. Why don't you walk down to the gate now and tell the woman we won't be riding with her? Don't reveal any more than you have to; maybe only that someone has been hurt and we're waiting for help to come. Hurry now, the police should be here soon. They'll want to talk with both of us."

"Henry, I need to hear what you say to them. Our stories must match or we're in trouble, so if they come before I'm back...."

"Keep my mouth shut?" He nodded. "Go on, Cara. They'll look at the victim and his surroundings before they bother much with us."

* * *

Trouble was, he agreed with her. He didn't want to become involved in this either. If she hadn't seen the man, they wouldn't be, so why couldn't he describe how they found the body and not mention the two men sitting in front of them on the train?

Back in Kansas City he'd had witnesses do that to him all the time. Citizens would tell the truth, but leave out stuff, sometimes intentionally, sometimes not. And, what was left out often slowed down or messed up investigations. Did retirement change him into that kind of citizen?

He puffed his cheeks, blew out air. No. Part of him would always be Police Major Henry King. Besides, speaking practically, if this man had come from the train, the police would learn that and, eventually, learn he had been sitting right in front of Carrie. What then?

No more time to think about it now. The Van Buren Police Department and a medical team van had arrived.

Two officers, both male, got out of the car. One was a sergeant, stocky and self-assured; the other was a tall skinny kid who looked weighted down by the equipment on his belt. *But,* Henry thought, *back when I began police work, I looked about like that kid.*

Sergeant Lonnie Burke introduced himself and Officer Julio Mendez, then listened to Henry's name. As soon as the medical technician had pronounced the victim dead, the sergeant squatted by the body, looking without touching. Then he turned back toward Henry, pointing to the pizza box. "You do this?"

"Yes. My wife and I checked to see if he might still be alive. The box was there, so I lifted his head out of the water and laid it on the box."

"Wife?" The man looked around.

"Yes. She'll be back soon. She went to tell the woman who planned to drive us back up the hill that we wouldn't be riding with her."

The young officer had stepped away to call for the help they'd need, but the sergeant kept looking at Henry, obviously expecting more.

"My wife was in the woman's shop, and they were talking about Van Buren history. The woman said we should see the mural in this park, said if we'd walk down here she could give us a ride back after she finished her lunch break. She lives on a boat somewhere in this area." He swept his arm toward the docks. "My wife was walking ahead of me and she saw this first." he gestured toward the body. "I came up a moment after."

"Ah, I see. Woman living on a houseboat? That would be Jenni Lively. So, why didn't you drive here yourself? Come in on the train?"

"Yes."

The sergeant nodded and looked back at the body. He began using his eyes and gloved hands to check the area round it while Henry looked toward the park entrance and saw Carrie almost running toward them. Well, he hadn't said anything to the police yet that she wouldn't corroborate naturally. It was the future that might get sticky.

She arrived, out of breath, looking hot and very bothered. The sergeant would think that natural, Henry decided as he introduced them, and Sgt. Burke said, "Let's talk while we're waiting for the forensics team. Ma'am, I understand you saw the body first."

"I had walked ahead of Henry, so I saw him first."

"You were here to look at the mural?"

"Yes."

"But you walked beyond the mural."

"Yes. I wanted to see more of the river and decided to go as far as the railway bridge there." She pointed. "I noticed trash along the river bank, and then saw what I initially thought was a big pile of rags caught at the water's edge. I walked closer, and...."

"And?"

"Saw it was a man."

"Do you recognize him?"

She hesitated only a moment. Then, looking straight at Sgt. Burke without even a side glance at Henry, she said, "Not really, but we came here on the excursion train and there were two men sitting in the seats in front of us. One of them had light blond hair and was wearing a blue shirt. I never saw his face."

So, Henry thought, *the die is cast. And good for her.*

"Okay. Now then, when you first saw the man here on the bank, did you touch him?"

"Yes, I touched him because I needed to find out if he was still alive."

"And?"

"I felt around in the water for his arm, lifted it up and

35

checked his wrist, but detected no pulse. I was going to try and lift his head away from the water next. You know, feel for a pulse in his throat and then see about expelling water if I could. But before I started that, Henry arrived. He lifted the head. When we saw the man's face and eyes, we could tell...."

Sgt. Burke pointed two indentations in the soft soil. "Are those footprints yours?"

"Yes. But the big one over there isn't."

"How about you, sir? That your footprint?"

"No. I stayed back as far as I could, and only stepped on the rock over there. Besides, my arms are longer than Carrie's. I could reach him without getting in the mud."

"How about on the train? Did you see him there, too?"

"I only saw the man's back. I must have been looking out the window when he came in and sat down."

"So neither of you can confirm whether or not this might be the same man?"

"No," they said in unison.

"You said there were two men sitting in front of you. Were they together?"

"They didn't come in together," Carrie said.

"So you don't know if they were acquainted?"

"No."

"What did the other man look like?"

"Dark hair," she said, "not overly long, but lots of it. Some silver scattered throughout his hair. Clean-shaven, pale skin, medium height, maybe weighed 175. Age, probably around fifty. Khaki pants, a black polo shirt. He carried a black tote bag. I saw his face when he came in the car, and I'm sure I'd recognize him again. I can't tell you the color of his eyes. He had on tinted glasses."

The sergeant studied her for a long moment before he said "Thank you. You're unusually observant." He turned to Henry. "And you?"

Henry spoke slowly, reflectively. "Most of the time the two men acted like strangers. However, a public television cameraman was in the car filming for a program, and I noticed both men strongly resisted appearing on camera. They both started to go to another car when that option was offered. However, though I didn't see them discussing it, they ended up deciding to stay in our car. Then they always found ways to conceal their faces when the cameraman was in their area. I didn't get as good a look at the man in the black shirt as my wife did, but I would probably recognize him too."

An unmarked black car drove toward them and, when Burke went to the roadside to meet the new arrivals, Carrie moved closer to Henry.

"It's okay?" she asked, as soon as the sergeant was out of earshot.

"It's okay. There was really nothing else we could do, and I am grateful to you for being such a trooper. I'm sorry our day is wrecked, Cara, but we can come back here another time."

"Did you tell those guys about your background in law enforcement?"

"Nope."

"Afraid they'd either want to depend too much on

you, or worry you were going to be in their way?"

"That's about it. You know how things have sometimes gone when we got involved with police officers in the past."

"What if they find out?"

He thought about it. "Well, not telling them what I retired from is hardly withholding important information. In fact, they'd probably be grateful I didn't tell them. Keeps things uncomplicated, or at least less complicated than they already are." He shut his eyes for a moment and opened them to stare out over the river, obviously seeing nothing.

She touched his arm. "I'm sorry Henry, so sorry. But you've always done what was right—what you had to do, back then and now."

He cleared his throat. "I just want... I want you, and Susan and her family, and Catherine and Rob, and all our friends to be safe and at peace. Y'know, I really thought life would be more peaceful when I moved from Kansas City to the Arkansas hills."

She nodded. "But that isn't exactly what happened once you met me, is it?"

"No, but JoAnne's murder certainly wasn't your fault. And since your detecting located my daughter, which also got me a grandson and son-in-law I didn't know existed, I can't really complain, can I? Then there's Catherine. I probably would never have met her in this life if you hadn't invited her to our wedding. As for Rob? He could be my own son. Like I said, I can't complain."

He smiled down at her, but felt unshed tears in his

eyes. He blinked, then took her arm. Together, they walked across the street to stand in the shade.

More people, including a woman who was probably the coroner, came. Two men began making a thorough search of the area and taking photos. Another joined Sgt. Burke by the body. Henry was itching to be over there on the river bank, and he supposed Carrie was too. It was more than curiosity. They'd found the body and had a right to be interested.

Burke stood and, holding what looked like a plastic sandwich bag in his hand, walked toward them.

"Did either of you look in his pockets?" he asked.

They both shook their heads.

"Any ideas about this?" He held out the bag, but pulled it back when Carrie instinctively reached out to take it.

"For goodness' sake," she said, "it's a sack of little ivory buttons. There must be more than two dozen in there. What on earth?"

"Mr King? Ever see these before."

"No. Peculiar things for a man to have in his pocket. Was he carrying a weapon, by the way?"

The sergeant hesitated for a moment, then said, "No."

"Can you tell us how he died?"

"Don't know for sure yet. He'd been stabbed several times, but it's likely he ended up drowning."

"I didn't see any defensive wounds on the hand I pulled out of the water," Carrie said.

"You noticed that?"

"Well, yes."

"Okay. He would have bled when he was out in the water. There's some current along the shore, so you prob'ly wouldn't have seen blood unless you came along on the tail of the killer. You didn't mention seeing any blood."

They both shook their heads, and Carrie said, "No blood."

"We haven't found a knife yet. But with a river to throw it in, well...."

Henry said, "Big playing field."

"You bet. That river conceals a lot of secrets."

"Sounds like you think he was killed here."

"Yes. Or maybe in a car that was parked close by. This isn't exactly a thoroughfare, but trucks and cars do come by occasionally, and people jog or walk from the park, so the killer would have had to be careful, or real lucky. Couldn't make too much fuss or he might be noticed. Boats docked down the river would most likely be empty this time of day, but that's no guarantee someone wouldn't see him."

Carrie looked down river. "The antiques shop lady was home for lunch. Can she see this area from whichever boat is hers?"

"Maybe. We'll check, but I think she'd have called us if she saw something."

Henry asked, "Did you find anything to indicate the dead man was on the train today?"

Burke squinted at him, said, "Who are—?" sputtered, stopped, and began again. "No, not yet. No ticket or flyers from the train. No wallet, either. No keys. Only buttons."

Carrie broke in. "Could he and the killer have been in a small boat? That clump of trees out in the water would have concealed them unless they came around toward the shore."

Burke looked startled, then chagrined. "I guess we haven't come to that idea yet. But you're right, it would have been much easier to hide the murder if it happened in a small boat; though, if the victim fought his killer, well–who knows–he could have swamped the thing. Still, a boat might have been noticed from out in the river, though it wouldn't be seen from shore if it was behind the island.

"Now, besides that, have you thought of anything else? How about if you noticed the man in the blue shirt leaving the train with anyone, or saw what direction he went from the station?"

Henry looked at Carrie. She shook her head, and he said, "No, sorry."

"Well, then, I'll just go talk to the guys for a moment, then I'll drive you up to the train. We're having it held, at least until we can interview the passengers."

Burke started away, then turned back. "Mr. King, I don't suppose you've ever been in law enforcement?"

"I'm retired from the Kansas City Police Department."

"Ah." He looked at Carrie. "And you?"

Before she could say anything Henry answered for her. "She's done a little investigating."

"Thought so," Burke said, and walked off.

Carrie put a hand over her mouth, and Henry saw that she was concealing a grin she couldn't stop. He said, "All that talking to people on the train is going to take a while."

"Uh-huh. Y' know what? Maybe we should have paid more attention to those two guys after all."

If it hadn't been so inappropriate for the current situation, he'd have snorted in fake disgust and then, probably, laughed out loud.

DOPPELGANGER

At least the police car didn't smell like dirty bodies and alcoholic vomit. In fact, Carrie thought as she slid across the plastic seat, it had almost no smell at all, and this was something to be grateful for. Sure, she and Henry were sitting behind metal screening, but she'd expected that, as well as the missing smell.

Half-way up the hill Sgt. Burke pulled into an open parking space, and Carrie, who'd been wondering what to do about the package she'd left behind in the antiques shop, said, "I bought some things at Lively's, and since you've stopped, could I go in and pick them up? It won't take a minute."

"Are they paid for?" Burke asked.

"Yes, of course," she told him, curious what business that was of his.

"Officer Mendez can get them for you. He needs to talk with Jenni Lively anyway; then he'll join us on the train."

"They're fragile. I bought crystal."

"Hear that Mendez? Handle Ms. McCrite's package with care."

Mendez grinned at her, gave a small salute, and headed into the store.

* * *

So, Henry thought, *they're checking to see if Carrie and I really were here in the upper part of Main Street until noon.*

Well, so what? He had no right to be offended. He'd

43

have done the same thing in their shoes.

On the other hand, maybe the police just wanted to ask Lively if she'd seen anything unusual during her lunch break. That might be it.

Carrie was staring at him with a quizzical look on her face. He supposed that meant she now realized they were suspects in a murder case, if she hadn't thought of it before. Well, it wasn't the first time she'd brushed close enough to death-by-intent to be a suspect. Being a suspect was, however, a new experience for him. He'd killed, oh yes, he'd killed twice, but in the line of duty.

He'd enjoyed his chosen profession. But to have a job where it could be your duty to kill? He hadn't thought about that too much until after the convenience store, when everyone said it had been his duty to kill a kid who'd already murdered at least one man.

His duty to kill.

If only he could erase that convenience store from his memory.

Carrie was still looking up at him, so he smiled at her, and reached out to take her hand.

* * *

They arrived to find a train as full of loud conversation as a classroom before the opening bell. The passengers were all seated, but that didn't keep them from discussing events and shouting back and forth to each other. A police officer moved along the aisle, writing down names and contact information, and checking drivers' licenses against what he was being told. A second officer spoke with conductors in the car's vestibule.

The only vacant seats remaining were at the front, across the aisle from seats marked "Reserved." Carrie wondered if that meant Chuck Dovish and the cameraman still planned to make the return trip.

After Carrie and Henry were settled, Burke went to confer with the officer taking information and–not caring how it looked–Carrie turned around and got on her knees to peer over the seat back. She wanted to see if Black Shirt was in the car.

Everyone seemed to be speculating about an accident on the river bank that possibly involved someone from the train, but no one paid any attention to Carrie as she began surveying the full car. The police must not have mentioned who discovered the "accident," and, so far, no one looked angry or impatient about the delayed departure.

Carrie checked her watch. It was only 2:30, not time to be impatient yet.

The conductors, released from their police questioner, began passing out drinks and snacks along the aisle. Carrie accepted a sack of Oreo cookies and a bottle of water and, munching a cookie, looked from seat to seat, inspecting occupants.

What the...? It couldn't be!

A blond-haired man in a blue Oxford cloth shirt sat right in front of where she'd been seated on the trip down. While she watched him in stunned surprise, the man took a swig of Pepsi and stared back at her, unblinking and unsmiling.

Feeling a decidedly uncomfortable chill, she switched her gaze away from Blue Shirt and began looking along the row of seats on the opposite side of the car, but didn't see anyone resembling Black Shirt. Well, he could be in the other car. She turned around, bumped back down in her seat, and gaped at Henry.

"What?"

"The man in the blue shirt...."

"What about him?"

"He's *here*, or I think he is. You look. Right where he sat on the way down."

"Are you sure?"

"Just look."

He did, sat silently for a moment, then said, "That means we have no clue to who the man on the river bank was, and are therefore completely out of this investigation."

"Guess so, but...."

"But nothing, Cara. We're out of it. Next thing you need to think about is what you're going to say to Chuck Dovish."

"Well...."

Burke appeared in the aisle next to them. "Officer Williamson says the conductor verifies that all of the passengers are accounted for, and I see a blond man in a blue shirt near the back of the car. Could that be the man who sat in front of you on the ride down?"

She said, "As you know, we didn't see his face, but yes, it must be the same man. He's even in the same seat."

Henry asked, "Did he say why he's here?"

"Sightseeing and experiencing a ride on the rails like everyone else. We're going to release the train. Seems it, and you, have nothing to do with our event on the river. As soon as Mendez gets here with your package and the TV people take their seats, you'll be on your way."

SHIRLEY BOOTH REMEMBERS

"What did the buttons look like?" Shirley asked.

She, her husband Roger, Jason and Eleanor Stack, and Carrie and Henry were seated around the heavy oak table in the Booth's kitchen. Plates showing only bits of piecrust had been pushed toward the table's center as Carrie and Henry told about their excursion train adventure.

"Tiny, like maybe for a child's dress. Ivory color. I realize they couldn't be real ivory since that would be illegal today. They had a dome shape and were no bigger than my little fingernail. They were sure cute. Cute as a... a button." She laughed.

"Hold up a minute," Shirley said. "Roger, you see to the water and coffee while I go look for something."

When she returned, Shirley leaned over the table and spilled three buttons onto the red-checked cloth. "Like these?"

"Oh, my gosh, yes." Carrie picked the buttons up, stared at them for a minute, then dropped them into Eleanor's outstretched palm. "They looked exactly like these. Where on earth did you get them?"

"From Gramma Moore, Mama's mama. She said her pa, who was a Bilford, brought a bunch of them home from Van Buren after he was through with soldiering. He gave them to his sister, Sarella, and their mama sewed a few of them onto Sarella's dresses. Aunt Sarella never had children, so she passed what hadn't been lost over the years on to Gramma. Kinda odd for war keepsakes, aren't they?"

"How did your great-grandfather get them in the first place?"asked Eleanor, handing the buttons on to Jason.

"Let Carrie finish her story about the trip first. Then I'll tell you Great-grampy Bilford's story."

"I was about done," Carrie said, "unless Henry has something to add. The police drove us up to the train, and the man in the blue shirt was there, very much alive, and sitting in the same place he'd been on the trip from Springdale. I guess we'll never know now who the man on the river bank was, or why he was killed. And that's the end of the story."

"That river has a lot of stories," Roger said, handing the buttons to Henry. "And the one Shirley's gramma told is a doozie."

Henry gave the buttons back to Carrie, and she arranged them in a triangle on the table top, then began pushing them around with her finger, remaking triangles among the table cloth squares, as Shirley began talking.

"Great-grampy went to war before he finished being sixteen. He was in the battle at Prairie Grove under Major General Hindman early in December of 1862, and —"

"Hold it, Shirley," Jason said. "We Yankees need a little help. Don't forget Eleanor and I didn't move here from Ohio until seven years ago. We've visited the Prairie Grove battlefield, but I don't remember the details now. I suppose your relative was in the Confederate Army?"

Shirley nodded.

"So, Hindman was the Confederate general? Who

won at Prairie Grove?"

"No one, really, though the Confederates prob'ly came out the worst. They had to withdraw from the area at night and hightail it for Van Buren. Hindman was a spikey sort of fellow, and he'd decided he could overcome the Union forces and drive on north into Missouri to make up for the Confederate loss at Pea Ridge back in March. When it didn't turn out that way, the air went out of his balloon, so to speak. He'd just been demoted because of unpopular decisions, and this new mess didn't help any. All told, over 2700 men died at Prairie Grove, and Hindman, who'd started with 11,000 men, retreated to Van Buren with less than 9,000. He lost around 1,300 in the battle and others deserted or were too sick to fight.

"Anyway, Great-grampy and the remainder of Hindman's men ended up at Van Buren, and to make a long story short, got the worst of a battle there right after Christmas. It was bitter cold, everyone was hungry, and his troops hadn't been paid, which made hardships for their families as well as them. As far as Great-grampy was concerned, war hadn't turned out to be the big adventure he expected, and he was ready to head home.

"Well now, there were several supply boats in the river near Van Buren at that time. Stories are told saying one of them had pay for the Confederate army on board, secured in an iron safe. Others had supplies for the army, and for towns and forts along the river, clear up to Ft. Gibson, in Oklahoma."

"Boats went that far up the river? I almost can't

believe it," Carrie said.

"It was tricky, and some got beached or hit snags, but they were small, flat-bottom boats so—at least in high water—most made it through.

"Well anyhow, three Confederate boats tried to escape down-river and got caught by the Federals. Great-grampy and others were sent by Hindman to off-load what supplies the army could use from two more boats still docked in town. When everything usable was off, they were ordered to set fire to the boats and sink them.

"Remember now, these soldiers were just kids. After the loaded supply wagons pulled away, the boys set fire to one of the boats, then decided to look through what was left on the other one before they finished following orders. Great-grampy carried away small things to bring home—a bunch of ivory buttons for Sarella, brass belt buckles for him and his pa, and some silver spoons for his ma. No one found any safe with money, and I can't see what those boys would have done with the safe had they found it. Anyway, they finally did bash holes in the second boat and set fire to it, but, according to stories passed down from Great-grampy, not much got burned before she went down. "

"So at least one fairly intact boat was sunk at Van Buren?" Jason asked.

"Yessir, and there were more over the years both before and after, mostly from hitting snags and other kinds of accidents."

"And they're still there? In the river?"

"Far as I know. Of course after the war, snag boats

worked to clear the river for traffic, and there have been lots of floods through time, not to mention that the locks and dams were added. I reckon no one knows where, what, or if, boats lie under that river now, though, with modern inventions, maybe a body could find them in the mud if any thought it worth their while."

"But since that dead man had buttons like yours in his pocket, maybe...." Eleanor began.

"Eggs-ackly" said Shirley, grinning around the table. "So, anyone for a trip to Van Buren? Who knows what we might find in the shops, not to mention along the river. And, haven't we all been saying we wanted to make a trip there together?"

"Do you want to take the train?" Henry and Carrie said in unison.

"No, not this time," Jason said. "We'll drive. Eleanor has been wanting to get to Van Buren again anyway, to see if she can find some unusual containers that will work for her flower arrangements. What do you think, Ell?"

"Yes, we'll take the Highlander from Eleanor's Flower Garden, and one or the other of you guys can drive, too. We'd have room for you going down, but if I find lots of good stuff we might not have room on the return. What about you, Roger? Can you get away?"

"We have a couple calves due soon, but after that just pick a day in September when Junior can handle the milking. Then Shirley and I are in. Okay, Mother?"

"You bet. It's time we had us another mystery to solve."

Henry held up both hands in mock horror. "This is just a sight-seeing and buying trip, right?"

"Right," said Roger and Jason.

"Uh-huh," said Carrie, Shirley, and Eleanor.

A TELEVISION SPECTACULAR

"Hey," Carrie said, opening the September AETN program guide, "next Monday's Exploring Arkansas program is called 'Historic Train Ride.' I'm sure that's us, but I'll phone the station to be sure before I start telling everyone."

Henry turned away from his computer. "Can we invite the Booths and Stacks here for supper that evening and watch the show together?"

"Oh. Well... um... let me think. Yes, I guess we can. I'll make that chicken casserole Dorothy served after church last spring. I got her recipe. She said it was easy to put together, and it doesn't look complicated. Roger will holler about using canned chicken instead of fresh, but if he wants fresh chicken he'll have to bring me six cups of white meat ahead of time, all cooked and cut up. I'm not about to face his hens on the hoof."

"Canned was fine for Dorothy's casserole, so don't worry about it," Henry said, "and how about a fruit salad? I'll fix brownies and ice cream for dessert."

"You're on. And be ready to record the program so we can share it with Rob and Catherine later."

"Yup, and Susan and her family," Henry said. Then he went back to searching the Internet for more information on heirloom tomato seeds for next summer's garden.

* * *

The canned chicken casserole vanished with praise, plus two helpings all around, and without comment from

Roger about the chicken's source. Everyone was ready for the program start by 6:25.

"I promise not to say anything during the program," Carrie said, "and if we're in it, don't you dare laugh at my comments. Just you face a television camera and see what comes out of your mouth. We can talk about the program after it's over. Don't forget to watch for Blue Shirt and Black Shirt. I'm curious to see if their faces ever show on camera."

"Me, too," Eleanor said. "I think we all are."

The show began with pictures of the Springdale station and the train, then the camera moved in to catch people boarding.

"Carrie, that's you!" Eleanor said.

"Sheesh, from behind, and looking like I'll never make it up those steps. Quick, everyone shut your eyes and don't you guys dare laugh."

At long last the camera swerved toward passengers waiting in line and Carrie said, "Okay, you can look again."

"Never stopped," whispered Jason, elbowing Roger in the side, and gaining annoyed glances from both Roger and Henry.

"Is that your blue shirt fella?" Shirley asked, "there, by the old baggage cart."

Carrie jumped out of her chair. "Henry, do you see? Isn't that... look, Henry, look at his face. It's the man on the river bank."

After that everyone talked at once until, several minutes later, Carrie finally spoke loudly enough to be heard over the din. "There's the blue shirt guy on the return trip, and something's funny about him. I definitely remember that the man going to Van Buren was tall, at least from the waist up. Before he started to scrunch down and hide his face, his shoulders were above the seat back. That's how we could tell the shirt color. Oh, drat. You missed him now, but as soon as this is over, we'll replay it and I'll show you."

Forty-five minutes later, Henry said, "I think you're right. It looks like the guy I'll call Blue Shirt Two is sitting up straight, and his shoulders still don't reach the top of the seat back. I'd say the face is different, too, though not in a major way. Hard to tell, since the camera was taping from the front of the car then. But the photographer caught that other guy on the platform close up. I'd bet Blue Shirt One never knew he was being recorded for posterity. Not that he'll care. I'm sure he's the man we found on the bank of the Arkansas River."

"The second man's hair is darker blond, too," Carrie said.

"I'll phone Sgt. Burke in the morning," Henry said. "We need to get a copy of the program to him, or suggest he order one from AETN. And that leads into our plans for a group trip to Van Buren. How soon can all of you go?"

"This Wednesday okay?" asked Roger.

"Fine," Jason said. "Let's meet in our driveway at 7:30."

* * *

Henry wasn't looking forward to the phone

conversation with Sgt. Burke. The sergeant hadn't been in touch with him since their day in Van Buren, and Henry, knowing he had no right to resent that, resented it anyway. "After all," he said to Carrie, "we might have thought of something important to add to his information, even if he didn't want to bring us up-to-date on the investigation. He should have respected our potential input."

"Yes, my love, but it's probably not his nature to share in that manner. He may even think of it as unethical." She stood on tip-toe to give him a kiss. "You know how police officers can be, right? He did give us his card, and I'm sure he thought we'd call him if we had any new information. And now, you are going to call him.

"That poor sergeant simply doesn't know how useful you might be to him, if only as a sounding board. It would be great if you two could talk over a cup of coffee and a piece of pie at Carol's, but that's not likely since we live a hundred miles away."

Still feeling resentful, and with Carrie hovering nearby, Henry dutifully called the Van Buren Police Station on Tuesday morning and asked for Sgt. Burke.

"He's out," the woman on the phone said, "May I find someone else to help you?"

Henry asked for Officer Mendez, was told he was off duty, and, after a moment's thought, said, "Perhaps if I explain my situation, you can put me in touch with the right person. But first, I'd like to know what progress there's been in the case of the body found on the riverbank in July. My wife and I are the ones who discovered him. We came in on the A&M passenger train that day, and at first it was thought the dead man did too. But we learned later that all passengers were accounted for on the return trip. Are you with me?"

"Yes," the woman said, "I know the case you mean."

"I have no authority to ask this, but something has come up that makes it important for me to know where you are on that case."

"I don't have that information. You'll have to—"

"Let me explain further. A representative from Arkansas Public Television filmed the train trip that day. The resulting program was shown on AETN last night. During the program my wife and I saw what we consider very important information pertinent to the murder. Has the case been resolved yet?"

"I'll get in touch with Sgt Burke at once," the woman said, still not answering Henry's question. "Where can he reach you?"

The sergeant returned Henry's call five minutes later.

"Willa says you have new information on the riverbank case."

Henry explained.

The man's pursed-lip intake of breath sounded like a failed whistle and revealed his interest. "I'll phone the TV station right away, and send someone there to pick up a recording of the program. You don't need to bother sending a copy to me."

Henry said, "We plan to be in Van Buren tomorrow. If we can meet and view the tape together, Carrie and I will point out what we saw."

"How about meeting me at the station at 10:00?"

"We'll be there. I assume then, that the case hasn't been closed."

"Nope. Going nowhere."

"Have you identified the dead man?"

"No such luck. He has no fingerprint record and there's no matching missing person report."

"That's tough. I'd like to hear more about it tomorrow, and I hope what we have to show you helps. I've also discovered something interesting about those buttons you found in the dead man's pocket."

"What about them?"

"A friend of ours had a relative in the December, 1862 Battle of Van Buren. He brought home buttons that look like the ones you found on the dead man. They've been passed down in her family, and she has them now. They came from one of the steamboats her great-grandfather and his buddies sank on the orders of Confederate Major General Hindman, but only after they did a bit of private requisitioning. That friend is coming with us tomorrow. Should I ask her to bring her buttons for comparison?"

"She know about this case?"

"Yes, fully. In fact, four of our friends know everything Carrie and I do, but they're all discreet, and familiar with police investigations. All of them will be with us tomorrow. We planned on searching the antiques shops to see if we came across anything that might possibly be salvage from a steamboat, and maybe take a look along the river as well."

"Hmmm. I guess I should tell you this, then. When we went to search the island just beyond where your wife found the body, we learned right away why no one goes there. It's unstable, a mushy mess. It looked to us like water had broken through, and made a fairly new wash clear into the center of the island. Probably did that during the spring floods. We couldn't get our boat in there, but wondered if a smaller boat might have made it. Officer Mendez is an adventuresome sort, and he put on waders to go in through the muck, holding onto tree branches above him to keep from sinking. Right in the middle of the island, at the end of an open wash, he says he saw what he thinks is the top of a smokestack, like might have been on a steamboat, you know?

"We've kept that quiet so far, not knowing if it made any difference in our case, and not wanting to attract scavengers or treasure hunters. As long as I've lived here, there have been rumors running around about Confederate silver that went down in a steamboat docked here during the Civil War. Money to pay the troops, you know. I always discounted it because there are dozens... maybe hundreds... of stories like that all over the South. Folks around here pretty much consider it no more than gossip, but now I'm beginning to wonder if there's some truth behind the local story."

"Ah," said Henry. "Mendez saw no sign anyone had dug, or poked around to see what was buried in the mud?"

"Nope, but all the unstable muck would probably wipe out any evidence of digging."

60

"Oh. Right."

"I'll see you tomorrow, then. I would like to have a look at those buttons. Go ahead and bring your friend to the station with you if she doesn't mind."

"You realize that means all six of us will be there?"

The sergeant's sigh was audible. "Well, why not? This case has gotten out-of-hand peculiar anyway."

WHO IS GORDON A. HAWKINS?

By the time Henry reached the Van Buren Police Station parking lot he was feeling like a reluctant scout leader. Now that the Booths and Carrie were out of his car, and standing with him in the parking lot waiting for Jason and Eleanor to join them, everyone–including Carrie–had adopted a "you tell us what to do next" demeanor. That flummoxed him.

His discomfort increased when all six of them crowded into the police station's small waiting room and the entire group, which seemed huge by now, hung back, waiting for him to approach the women behind the protective glass and ask for Sgt. Burke.

The sergeant appeared at once, and greeted Henry like an old friend, which melted his remaining unhappiness over being sidelined earlier. *I was being stupid,* he thought. *I'm retired, period. I wouldn't feel resentment about a police officer not treating me as a confidante if I was a retired accountant or auto mechanic. I have no right to feel left out because I'm a retired police officer instead.*

Then a new thought surprised him. *Whoa, Henry King. No matter how much you insist to Carrie that you're glad to be done with police work, that's not entirely true, is it? Therefore, in all honesty, quit acting like a balky jackass when Carrie wants the both of you to help people in trouble.* He smiled as a modern chastisement for his attitude popped into his head.

Get over it.

He became aware that Sgt. Burke had just asked, "Any of you carrying?" and was being answered by a blank look from Eleanor and shaking heads or "No," from the rest of the group. Carrie whispered a quick explanation to Eleanor, who's eyes widened into surprised circles.

Coming back to the present, Henry said, "None of us," and Burke, taking over as scout leader, guided them into a small conference area, saw that they were seated, and offered coffee, which everyone but Henry refused.

Must have something to do with my jokes about police station coffee, Henry thought as he tested the Van Buren Police coffee, which was actually quite good. He looked at his watch. By ten in the morning any remaining brew in the KC coffeepot would have been growing stouter for at least six hours. At least it used to be that way.

"Your coffee is very good," he told Sgt. Burke, and watched the surprised looks on his friends' faces.

When no one changed their mind about coffee, the sergeant said, "We got the program from the TV station and can watch it now. Officer Gregory will run it for us. Just give a holler when you want the tape stopped to point out something."

Before long Carrie and Henry both said "Stop" and the picture froze on the face of a man standing by the antique baggage cart at the Springdale depot.

"There." Henry got to his feet and went to put a finger on the television screen. "That face. Look familiar?"

"Anyone here squeamish?" the sergeant asked. When all shook their heads, he took photos from a folder spread and spread them on the table. "What do you think?"

They all looked. No one showed a sign of queasiness.

Real troopers," Henry thought.

Finally Roger spoke. "Same fella," and everyone nodded.

"Okay, let's finish the tape."

When the return trip segment began and Blue Shirt Two showed up on the screen, the program was halted again and everyone looked from the man in the railway car to the photos in front of them.

"They brought in a ringer," Roger said.

"Now we have to figure out who—and why," Burke said. "Okay Gregory, you can turn off the TV. Thanks."

The sergeant turned toward Shirley. "Major King said you had buttons to show me. How about we take a look at those now."

Shirley laid her three buttons on the table and the sergeant put the plastic sack from the dead man's pocket next to them. He opened the sack, removed a button, looked at it front and back, then rubbed it with his finger. He did the same with one of Shirley's buttons. Without comment he passed both buttons along the table.

Copying Burke, everyone performed the test he'd initiated, then Shirley spoke for all of them. "They're kin, but my buttons are a tiny bit darker, and they feel rougher somehow. Could the ones from the riverbank be plastic? I s'pose my old ones were made by hand and newer ones would be done on some kind of machine? Or could be they're both old and just came from different factories. I never heard where my family buttons were made." She hesitated. "Should we test more of them?"

Another set of buttons was handed around, then all heads nodded. "They are slightly different," Eleanor said.

Watching his friends take the matter of button judging so seriously filled Henry with gratitude and pride. Once more he thought, *They're real troopers.*

"Okay, thanks for your help," the sergeant was saying. "I don't know what these buttons mean, but they're at least interesting.

"Now, if you folks don't mind, I'll get our lists of passengers who rode the train that day and see if you recognize any names there. Of course, someone wanting to commit a criminal act prob'ly would have given the wrong name, but it could be some name will connect with at least one of you. We have two lists, the passenger list from A&M, and the list Officer Williamson made in the train. He checked them both and found the name of Blue Shirt on both lists."

"What was the name?" Henry asked.

"Gordon Hawkins," the sergeant said. "But, of course we can see now that the name must have been faked by Blue Shirt on the return trip."

Carrie asked, "How could he get away with that? Didn't everyone on the train have to show their driver's license to your officer?"

"Yes, but there was no identification on the man in

the river, so now it looks like the guy on the return trip could have had the dead man's billfold with his driver's license. They look enough alike for that to pass, which means there would be at least one fake name on one of the lists."

"Of course," Carrie said, "I should have thought of that."

Henry smiled at her sympathetically, then turned to Sgt. Burke. "Sounds like you verified the information on that license."

"It showed an address in Kansas City, and when Officer Williamson asked the second guy if that was his address he said yes. The Kansas City Police told me it is a real address, but the family living there now never heard of our guy, and they'd lived in the house for about a year. Hawkins wasn't the name of the family who sold them the house a year ago either. Records also show a Gordon Hawkins operated a souvenir shop in an area of the city called Museum Square. That area is full of museums, shops, and restaurants in restored old buildings, according to the officer I talked to. When K.C. Police checked the shop in July it was closed and a neighbor said the owners were on vacation. We asked the police to check the place for us again a couple of weeks ago, and the space was empty. After we heard that, we looked for bank records. Two accounts, both cleaned out and closed in August. Couldn't find credit cards issued to that name. There is a social security number, but it has the same address as the driver's license. Records showed Gordon Hawkins married a Danielle Buchanan some fifteen years ago. No record of a divorce."

"Tough," Henry said, "and Missouri drivers' licenses are good for six years. He could have moved several times during that period."

"Yup, could have, and you betcha it's tough." Burke grimaced. "Well now, I'll get those lists. Gregory, would you see if anyone here wants coffee now? I think Heatherman came in a bit ago and he always starts a new pot."

This time they all accepted coffee, and after the officer left to get it, everyone turned toward Henry. "What should we do next?" asked Jason. "How can we really help? Is this going to be one of those cases that's never solved?"

"All I can say is I hope it gets solved," Henry told him. "As for what we do next? I would like to look at the river bank again before I start surveying shops. Anyone else interested in that?"

"I think we all want to see the scene of the crime, don't we?" Eleanor said, looking around the table.

"You bet," Shirley agreed, as Officer Gregory came in with a coffee pot and cups, followed closely by Sgt. Burke with a file folder in his hand.

"Okay, we'll see if any of you folks might recognize a name here. According to Williamson, both lists have the same names. Heck, I know it's grabbing at straws, but maybe there's someone here you've heard of or know well enough to ask them about the trip and find out if they saw anything interesting, like did they notice if that guy in the blue shirt left with anyone? A&M says they always have passengers from your area, so it's just possible someone might be familiar to you."

"And you say Gordon Hawkins is on both lists?" Henry asked.

"Yes. And Williamson wrote down "blue Oxford cloth shirt" by the name of the guy on the return trip, because we expected a man like that to be missing. Now, let's see...." His finger moved quickly down the second list. "And here it is again, Gordon Allen Hawkins came into the station to buy his ticket the Wednesday before departure. Paid cash, but he did sign the register. Too bad we can't see that driver's license again and compare signatures. Well anyway, the name is the same on both lists."

He passed the second list to Henry and gave the first to Jason, who was sitting across from him. "Take your time looking, then pass them on."

No one said anything as the lists went to Carrie and Eleanor, and then on to Shirley and Roger. After a moment Shirley said, "Roger, see here, isn't that the name of the snooty guy at the bank? You know, the one who didn't think I had the brains or authority to sign papers for a loan when we built the new milking barn?"

Roger looked. "No, the bank fella's name is Dave, not Don, but...well, whada ya know?" His finger, showing a healing cut and permanently ground-in work dirt, tapped first his list, then Shirley's. "The name right above that."

Shirley looked. "Well yes," she said, sounding a bit impatient. "It's that blue shirt fella and...oh my lord-amercy, I get what you mean. It's someone who can't spell his own name. He's spelt it *A-l-a-n* on my list, and *A-l-l-e-n* with two *l*'s and an *e* on yours." She shoved both papers across the table to Burke and pointed. "See there?"

After a minute Burke lifted his head and said, "Don't know what it means yet, but the man who made the trip reservation, the man who ended up dead on the river bank, sure didn't spell his name the same as his...or rather *the* driver's license shows it. I wonder if that means he was the ringer, and not the second man, the one who's still alive, as we've assumed? I'll double-check with Williamson, as well as with the people who took reservations at the train station, but that's sure what it looks like. The driver's license that says *A-l-a-n* wasn't the dead man's to begin with. And now I wonder which of those two is from Kansas City, or maybe if they both are... were."

Henry said, "Looks like the guy on the return trip is from Kansas City, unless he was carrying the dead man's wallet."

Burke stood. "Things don't get easier, do they? Well, at least we have a couple new things to look into, thanks to you folks. Let us know if you think of anything else."

Thus dismissed, the group moved toward the door, but Henry stayed behind and said to Burke, "Will it be okay to give the Booths and Stacks details you previously shared with Carrie and me about that island and the smokestack Mendez saw? Since Shirley Booth has past family connections here, she might also have helpful information she doesn't realize is relevant yet."

"Oh, go ahead," Burke said. "But I still don't want gossip about any of this to get out around here. We'd probably have people swarming all over that mucky island or trying to get a small boat through to the center, and we aren't sure there isn't still information to help our case in there, though who knows what it might be? We've given up on finding that knife, by the way."

"Did you get word how Hawkins actually died?"

Doc says he was knifed first and, with no one to help him, would have bled out, but he did have water in his lungs. He was either under water, his face was shoved there, or he was too weak to lift his head above water level. He actually died by drowning in river water."

"Another question. What was the name of the man in the black shirt?"

"Oh, yeah, I intended to tell you that since you said you were going to check the Main Street shops. With all this other stuff, I forgot. He's Chandler Wilcox, and you might well run into him today. He lives in Van Buren and owns one of the shops you'll be looking into. He seems legit, been in business several years. Says he didn't know Blue Shirt, and never saw him before they sat together on the ride down."

"Why was he on the train?"

"Rode north the day before the murder to see a fellow antiques dealer in Fayetteville. Guy picked him up at the station on Friday, and they spent some time in his friend's shop. He stayed with the friend overnight, and rode back down here the next day."

"Interesting," Henry said. "We'll look for him this afternoon."

For a moment there was an awkward silence, as if both men were trying to think of what to say next. Henry looked at his feet, suddenly feeling a warm connection with this man and his job. Finally, he said, "Well, thanks, Sergeant. I'll be in touch if we come up with something helpful. And, would it be okay if I check back with you in a few days to see how things are going?"

"Sure, be my guest. And thanks again for your help. Good thing you saw that TV program."

They shook hands, and Henry went to join his friends.

THE *SARAH ANNE*

The two cars found their way from the police station to Main Street and thence downhill to the river. After both Jason and Henry had parked by the boat dock, everyone spilled out and walked to the bank. All of them were silent as they watched a towboat pushing six barges rumble past, headed down river.

"Who-ee, that's something to see," Shirley said. "Wonder what's in those things?"

"Prob'ly grain from the port at Catoosa over in Oklahoma," Roger said. "I've read about it."

Shirley looked around. "Okay. Well, down to business. Now, where did you find that dead man? You said you were looking at the mural?"

Carrie pointed. "Yes. I saw him a bit beyond the beginning of the mural. Up there, near the railway bridge. Do you want to walk? The park has a concrete walkway along the river."

Jason said, "I'll walk. I need to stretch my legs, and I can see the whole mural that way." He suited action to words, and the others hurried along behind.

"Nice park," Eleanor said as they passed over a foot bridge with brick pillars and wrought iron railings. "Too bad this pretty bridge goes over a junky wastewater gully."

"You're right," Carrie told her. "I'd sorta forgotten what it was like."

"Finding a dead body might could make you forget," Shirley said.

Henry led them a few feet beyond the end of the brick-trimmed walk and out onto an area of packed dirt and patchy grass. "There." He pointed. "He was half in, half out of the water. The ground is dry now. We can go closer."

They clustered together on the shore while Henry described, once more, what he and Carrie had seen and done that day. Then he told them what Officer Mendez had found in the center of the island that was now only a few yards from the shore.

Roger whistled. "You reckon, after all these years, Great-grampy Bilford's steamboat has come to daylight?"

"Roger Booth, you know it wasn't his boat, he just took stuff off and sunk it."

"Oh, I know that, but to me it's the Bilford Boat. That's what the kids called it when you told 'em the story, so I can call it the Bilford Boat if I want. I don't reckon we ever heard its real name."

"*Sarah Anne*. She was named the *Sarah Anne*."

"Too bad to sink a boat with such a pretty name," Eleanor said.

"War does that," Jason murmured.

"I know, I know, but it is a pretty name."

"Well, you've seen the place. Any thoughts?" Henry asked.

"My thought is we need a small boat," Roger said.

"Sgt. Burke wouldn't thank us if we poked around out there," Henry told him.

Carrie spoke up. "Have any of you seen traffic along

this road while we've been here? We did see a jogger on the path that day, but no other humans."

"And I've got a small boat," Roger said. "So small it fits in the back of our camper truck. The kids used it to play in our crick."

"They had good times in that boat you made," Shirley said.

"Yup," Roger agreed.

Everyone fell silent as an old pick-up parked behind them and a couple carrying fishing gear walked toward the shore several yards downstream.

After nods and smiles all around, Eleanor said, "Well, let's get some lunch, then go shopping. Shall we stick together or split up? I'm looking for interesting containers for plants and flower arrangements, and all of us will be looking for anything that might be as old as the Civil War and could be part of a cargo from the *Sarah Anne* or some other steamboat. Are we assuming there would be enough value in a cargo like that to cause a murder? It seems preposterous."

Henry said, "Remember, there is gossip about payment for the troops that was on some boat."

"Save your Confederate money, honey, the South will rise again," Jason chanted, laughing."How long would that money have lasted underwater and, except as a curiosity, what value would Confederate bills have now, anyway?"

"The gossip says it was all in silver coins," Carrie reminded him. "The soldiers needed money they could spend here and farther north. Silver fits that."

Roger spoke slowly, thinking aloud. "Well now, maybe it doesn't matter if there really is silver coin in the river or not. There's enough stories about that sort of thing everywhere around the South to make someone believe it. Confederate gold. Confederate silver. What someone believes is all that matters. Say you come to me, tell me you know where there's a huge amount of money in a sunk boat, but you need help to get at it. It's gonna take money to find money, right? Maybe you show me buttons you say came off that money boat, and I buy your story. What then?"

Shirley said, "Shoot. You might be able to get a little bitty boat into that island without anyone paying you mind, but if you get going on anything large enough to find a steamboat, then all the people living in Van Buren plus a bunch more would be on the shore watching you. You wouldn't get to keep the money anyway, would you?"

Roger rolled on, speaking more rapidly than normal now. "But say you never had the thought to salvage anything a'tall. Say it was a made-up story to get someone to dump money into your phony scheme. Say that person found out it was a... a hoax. What then?"

"He'd be mighty angry," Jason said.

"Right. Or maybe you say you got diving gear and can get into that boat from underwater where no one's gonna see you. How about that? The *Sarah Anne* maybe has holes bashed in her side already. Say you tell your patsy you can get in, quiet-like from underwater. That sounds like something a fella might believe. What do you think?"

Henry was staring at Roger. "Yes, believing it would be human nature, especially if the hearer was greedy. Greedy people dreaming of riches don't always think straight. They focus on the goal. It's like burglary. No one catches all the *what-if's*. Let's say burglars know how to dismantle the jewelry store alarm system and security cameras. They plan to come in at night. They've scouted the place, know the windows are barred, but see that the doors aren't. What they don't know is that barred gates close across the doors if a disturbance sets them off at night. I actually saw something like that happen in Kansas City. The burglars were caged like zoo lions. The dream of wealth blinded them and shut off reason. Happens to we humans all the time, whether it's robbery, shady stock deals, shady accounting, shady loan schemes, whatever. It's the hypnotism of 'get rich quick.'

"So, I see what you're aiming at Roger, and it could have happened something like you say. What's more I bet–because of the buttons and smokestack–that Burke will soon realize the possibility himself. I'll leave that alone for a while and see if he does."

"I still want to see inside that island," Roger said. "I'm just plain curious. And, in a way, it is sort of our family boat, no matter what my woman says." He held up a hand as Shirley aimed a swat toward him, and they both laughed.

Henry chuckled with them. "It's a hare-brained scheme Roger, and what do you hope to gain?"

"Riches?" He laughed. "Naw, but maybe I'll be able to touch Great-grampy's boat."

"Don't know what boat it is yet," Shirley put in. "May never know."

"You guys are all nuts, "Carrie said, omitting the comment that she, too, would like to see the center of that island. "Let's leave this, at least for now, get some lunch, and go shopping like Eleanor says."

"Reminds me," Henry said. "Burke told me the man, Chandler Wilcox, who wore the black shirt on the train, owns an antiques shop on Main Street. He didn't say which one, but, if the man is in his shop today, Carrie and I will be able to identify him. Let's stick together. If we're in a group, the fact that two people he might recognize from last July's train ride are looking around in his shop wouldn't seem as suspicious as if we were alone. Of course that's assuming he's involved in July's happenings, and I have a gut feeling he is. Anyway, we can take an especially close look at his stock, though all of us must be careful not to let on we know or care who he is. We're just shoppers and tourists, enjoying the town."

Eleanor said, "So, let's go shopping. But first, where's that Carol's restaurant you raved about, Carrie?"

IN THE FLEA MARKET

Since Eleanor and Jason often ate in restaurants much fancier than either Carrie and Henry or the Booths ever chose, Carrie cherished a frisson of pleasure when it became obvious both of the Stacks were thoroughly enjoying Carol's plain little café. They gobbled their plate lunches, then ordered pie with ice cream. It was almost as if they'd forgotten the importance of the afternoon shopping expedition.

Carrie hadn't. She'd killed time by making a trip to the Ladies', but Eleanor and Jason were still eating pie when she finally said, "If you all are finished, shall we start checking into the antiques stores? We have a lot of places to cover. Eleanor, Jason, you two are more familiar with shops along Main Street than the rest of us. Any suggestions?"

"Mmf, 'scuse me, just one more bite," Eleanor said. When she had wiped her mouth, she continued, "Let's start down hill from here, cover this side of the street until shops run out, then come back up on the other side, cross at the train station, and work our way back here to our cars. Since we're only interested in antiques, that will rule out a few of the places and save some time."

"Let's get started, then," Carrie said. "Everyone ready?"

"Potty stop first," said Eleanor, and slid out of the booth.

At last everyone was finished with necessities, and they were on the sidewalk heading for the nearest shop.

"How will you signal we're in the place owned by that fella who was on the train?" Roger asked.

"Good question," Henry said, "We can, uh–

Carrie broke in. "Henry and I will separate as soon as we enter a shop. When one of us calls out, 'Honey, come look at this,' that means we've seen him."

"Cool," Eleanor said.

From then on it was heavy shopping for Eleanor. By the time they'd been in four shops Jason had made several trips back to the Highlander to stow biscuit tins, baskets, crockery, and honest-to-goodness vases.

Carrie had to keep from staring in shock as her sophisticated friend presented a business card from Eleanor's Flower Garden as soon as they got inside a shop door, then, almost whispering, she wheedled and bargained with dealers, and was usually successful in getting at least a fourth knocked off prices. Just now she was murmuring, "How about fifty percent off if I buy everything on that shelf?" which Carrie thought outlandish until the dealer agreed, and began packing stacks of stoneware as fast as Eleanor could carry them to the counter.

Whew. And Carrie hadn't bought a thing, though Shirley found an old-fashioned hand-operated egg beater she said her youngest daughter would appreciate. "She's tried more'n once to get mine away from me," Shirley explained, as they moved down the street to the next shop.

This shop window could do with a cleaning, Carrie thought, as she led the way inside. The sales area was divided into sections, more like a flea market than a regular retail shop. When she noticed the merchandise varied widely from section to section, she decided her guess had been correct. A flea market for antiques.

There was no attendant at the counter, but in a minute a man hurried up from the back, explaining he'd been getting a bite of lunch.

"We just had lunch ourselves," Jason said. "Why don't you bring the rest of your food up front? It's okay with us if you finish while we look around. Right, gang?"

Those closest to the counter said, "Right," and the man looked at each of them, smiling until he saw Carrie. The smile broke for only a second, but in that second Carrie knew he had recognized her.

The group spread out to browse. Carrie and Shirley stayed together, moving along the aisle farthest from the counter. Seeing a weird-looking brass monkey on a top shelf, Carrie said, "Shirley, you're tall enough to reach the top shelf. Would you mind getting that monkey down for me to see?"

"Sure enough," Shirley said, giving Carrie a puzzled look as she handed her the figure.

"Honey, come look at this," Carrie called loudly, though Henry was only one aisle away. In a minute five people were crowded around Carrie, staring at the brass monkey.

"That man even has on a black shirt," Jason whispered. "The minute I saw him I wondered if he was the one."

Eleanor winked at Carrie and lifted her voice.

"Carrie, I don't think that will fit in the area you're thinking of." Then she added under her breath, "And it's the ugliest thing I ever saw."

"Oh, dear. Would you put it back for me, Shirley? Thanks. Now, all of you look around carefully. Keep your eyes open for something that will do in that spot. Holler if you see a possibility."

Roger murmured, "Seems we're already hollering. And are we thinking about a real spot, or a made-up spot?"

"Made-up. But how about picturing something about fifteen inches tall and not too big around."

They split into couples and began searching the store again. As soon as Carrie and Henry were a safe distance from the counter she said, "Chandler Wilcox. He recognized us, and didn't look pleased."

"You think so?"

"I'm sure. You weren't as close to him as I was. I could see his face clearly. He was not happy to see me."

"Interesting. That increases my feeling he's somehow connected to that victim on the bank."

They moved along in silence for a couple of minutes. Then Henry said, "Looks like these booths are stocked by different people. We might not find anything Wilcox himself has for sale... assuming, of course that he–or anyone else–really is salvaging from boat wreckage."

"Most flea market owners keep a few booths for their own merchandise, so—"

Shirley's voice rang out from two aisles away. "Carrie, I've found something you might like."

Once more six people clustered in a booth. "Lookie here," Roger said, pointing at items inside a locked glass-top box. "Our little buttons."

Shirley glanced up the aisle, then grabbed a tall glass bottle from a shelf above the button box. "How about this? You could put flowers in it. That would fill the space."

"It's a pretty bottle," Carrie said. "I like the bluish color. How much is it."

"Mmmm, ticket says twenty dollars."

"Is it old?"

Shirley surveyed both sides of the tag as the man in the black shirt walked up to them. "Doesn't say."

"It's quite old," Chandler Wilcox said, his expression neutral as he looked at Carrie. "I should have put that information on the tag. I found it at an estate sale. I don't know a date, but everything I bought was at least fifty years old. I think this is much older, though. Probably 1860's."

"I like it, but I was hoping for a single object that would work, not something I had to put flowers in to fill the space. I think I'll keep looking."

"I have an idea," Wilcox said. "Is your home formal?"

"Not at all. It's a log home."

"Ah. Give me a moment, then. There's some new stock in the back that isn't on display yet." He went down the aisle and disappeared into the back of the store, returning quickly with a hand full of bead and button flowers supported on green wire stems. Each stem also held a few glass leaves. He slid the stems into the bottle, poked at the flowers a bit, then stood back and said, "What do you think? You just blow or wash the dust off. No watering real flowers. No silks getting dingy."

Carrie smiled involuntarily. "They're wonderful, but I saw buttons like these in that case over there. They're marked eight dollars each, so I'm sure I can't afford your button flowers."

"Oh, those buttons are old. These are new copies. I find buttons and beads for a craftswoman in a small town near here, and she makes these flowers for me. I can sell you the bouquet for fifty dollars, and I'll reduce the bottle to twelve. It needs to be filled with clear florist's marbles to give it enough weight to support the flowers, but I'll throw those in for three dollars. That makes it sixty-five dollars for the lot."

"Sold," said Carrie.

"Well, I never," Shirley huffed.

Everyone was silent for a moment, then Shirley spoke again, pointing to the locked box. "So, where did these old buttons come from? They sure are expensive for little bitty buttons. What's the story, and how can you tell what's new and what's old?"

Wilcox hesitated only a moment. "The old ones are slightly different from the new. I don't know the exact source for the old buttons, but the person who sold them to me said they'd been in his family for at least a hundred years. Said he was clearing out his parents' home and found them in a sewing box that belonged to his great-grandmother. I liked them, and may have paid more for them than I should have." He shrugged, eyeing first Shirley, then Carrie.

"I like them too," Shirley said. "Where do the new ones come from then?"

"Wholesaler," the man said quickly, and, carrying bottle and flowers, he headed back toward the front counter, ending the conversation.

They spent another thirty minutes looking around the shop, but no one called the others to another viewing of suspicious objects, and eventually they left the store, telling the owner they had more looking to do and would return for Carrie's package in about two hours.

As soon as they were out on the sidewalk and headed down hill, Jason said, "I guess that was a bust, at least as far as learning anything of importance goes. What he said sounded plausible."

Carrie shook her head. "He could have been lying about a lot of the information he gave us. I can't wait to see my button flowers side-by-side with Shirley's old buttons. We know Shirley's are old because we can trace them back through her family. I assume it's true that the ones I bought are new, and, if comparing the buttons means anything, the ones Burke has are probably new, too. I wonder where the new ones came from."

"Hmpf, probably China," Shirley said. "Kinda makes me mad to see Great-grampy's buttons copied by new stuff. Sorry, Carrie, but that's the way I feel."

"I understand, but I think copying something can be a form of honor. Means it's worth reproducing, doesn't it?"

"Well, maybe. But I kinda liked owning something special."

"We should've bought at least one of those supposed old buttons back there," Roger said. "Compare the maybe old ones from the shop, Carrie's maybe new ones, and Shirley's for sure old."

As they reached the door of the next shop, Jason said, "You folks excuse me. I'm going back to buy two or three of those old buttons. Then we'll all have some to compare."

"Hmpf," Shirley said again.

Henry had been silent through this and now looked thoughtful. "I think we should return to the police station and tell Sgt. Burke about our find. Then we'll be able to compare all the buttons we know about. Let's all go back with Eleanor and Jason. They can buy buttons and Carrie can pick up her package."

* * *

Chandler Wilcox was still behind the counter when the group walked in. He was talking in normal tones with a blond-haired man standing at the counter. The two of them were looking at an object the newcomer held. Wilcox stopped in mid-word when he saw them, spoke softly to his customer, and turned away as if dismissing him.

The newcomer didn't look around. Pocketing whatever it was the two men had been discussing, he walked quickly to the back of the store and disappeared through a door.

Carrie, hoping she'd managed to conceal her

surprise, understood from Henry's squeeze on her hand that he, too, recognized the newcomer. She walked to the counter and said, "We decided we're all getting tired and want to head for home, so I'm back early to pick up my package."

Jason and Eleanor, paying no attention to any of them, headed toward the booth with the buttons. Black Shirt handed Carrie her package so quickly she almost dropped it. She managed a smile and a "Thank you," before she and Henry, with the Booths, left the shop.

"Ooops," Carrie said. "What do you make of that?"

"What's up?" Shirley asked.

Henry led the way along the sidewalk until they were several yards from the shop entrance, then he said, "The newcomer in the shop is the second blond man from the train, the one we decided was the real Gordon A. Hawkins. I hope it doesn't take the Stacks long to buy their buttons. We need to tell Burke about this as soon as possible."

"Call him on your cell phone," Carrie said. "Remember, the box with the buttons was locked, so Eleanor and Jason will have to get help from Wilcox, and that takes time. I wonder if their interest in those buttons will awaken more interest in all of us, assuming he really did recognize Henry and me, of course."

"Well now," Shirley said, glancing back down the sidewalk. "Who'd-a thought a few little bitty buttons would cause so much trouble."

"I'm sure there's no reason to worry about trouble. At least not for us," Henry said.

"Oh, I dunno. Blondie just came around the corner and got in a car down the street a piece. S'pose he wants to follow us–see where we're headed next? It's a blue Ford. I'll keep looking along the street like a gawking tourist and let you know if he pulls away or just sits there. Or, maybe I can look in this shop window and catch a reflection of his car."

"Interesting," Henry said. "Okay, keep watching. I'll go on ahead to our car and call the sergeant from there, where it won't be so obvious. Carrie, you come with me. Roger and Shirley, when the Stacks get back, explain the situation and bring them to our car."

"What about keeping an eye on that guy?" Shirley asked.

"We'll have to assume, if he hasn't left by the time the Stacks get here, that he's either going to follow us or go back in the shop as soon as we're safely out of the way. If he's still here when we're ready to leave, Jason and Eleanor can drive straight to the police station. Our car is more generic than their Highlander, so maybe Blondie won't easily recognize what I'm driving. I'll wait a bit to see if he follows the Stacks, then circle around the block. If he isn't in his car then, I'll assume he's gone back in the shop. But first, we'll see what Burke wants to do."

* * *

As soon as he and Carrie were seated in the car, Henry dialed the station. Evidently Burke was catching up on paperwork, because he answered the phone quickly. Henry explained about the buttons and the blond man in the blue Ford.

"You're over by Wilcox's shop?" the sergeant asked.

"Yes, parked in front of a shop called 'Happy Hobbies.' The blue Ford is a couple of doors south of the south edge of the flea market. Same side of the street. Shirley saw the blond man get in the car, I didn't."

"Okay. Give me ten minutes, I'll check. Stay there until I tell you to come to the station. What's your cell number?"

Henry told him, closed his phone, then repeated what Burke had said.

"Henry King, you actually ordered me to come back to the car with you. Should I put that down to an urge to keep me out of this? Or what?"

"Safety measure. I'm afraid it's my years of police work showing up. I'm trained to look for the slightest hint of danger. That's saved lives more than once, and I can't think of a life I cherish more than yours."

"Back at you," she said, reaching out to take his hand. "Remember bench seats, when a couple could really snuggle up in a car? I miss those."

He laughed. "That's one reason these bucket seats are safer. No distractions for the driver."

"So, do you think Roger and Shirley or the Stacks are in danger?"

"Carrie, if I did, I'd have warned them. We're the ones Chandler Wilcox and Hawkins have seen before. You can tell Wilcox, at least, is not dumb, so he must be wondering about now what we're doing here in Van Buren."

"Uh-huh." She had just laid her hand on his thigh

when Roger and Shirley opened the back doors to get in and Eleanor and Jason leaned in the windows.

"What's up?" Jason asked.

Henry told them, then said, "Burke's going to call me back. I'm sure he plans to...." He glanced in his side mirror. "I see his car back there now. He's gotten out to talk with our Gordon Hawkins. You two get in your car quickly and read maps or something. Don't look toward the police car."

"Aye, aye, captain," Jason said. "We're under cover, right?"

"Oh, for crying out loud, Jason, I'm serious."

But Jason and Eleanor were already headed for their car.

"That man is going to know one of us called the police," Carrie said.

"Can't help it. And, I'm sure Burke is cagey enough to simply say we recognized him from the train and, because he is so similar in looks to the dead man, he'd like to ask him a few questions. Or something"

"Or something," echoed Carrie.

THE BENEFITS OF CONVERSATION

While the four of them waited to see what the police car and the blue Ford would do, they bounced ideas around about what the dead man had been up to that got him killed. As far as Carrie was concerned, their ideas only made the situation murkier. Nothing at all seemed clear to her—not motive, nor goal, nor who was a killer, let alone what each of the three men was accountable for, though Roger's idea about a scam based on a bogus boat cargo seemed reasonable enough.

Roger's next words echoed her thoughts. "How about the fake treasure idea? Otherwise it sure makes no sense, trying to figure out who did what and why. It's a good thing I went into dairy farming instead of being a cop. At least I pretty much know what to expect from my cows."

Henry answered with what sounded like a chuckle, then said, "Police work can be tedious, and of course there is a lot of ugly stuff. But, most of the time you're doing research, talking to people, thinking about all facets of a case and the people involved, following every possible clue. You keep chipping away, and hope something will eventually break loose."

"That so?" Roger said. "Okey dokey, I'm chipping away. Who is this Gordon Alan-Allen Hawkins? Is he a killer? Inventor of a shady scheme? Look-alike to throw someone off kilter?"

"Careful Roger, you're starting to think like a cop," Henry said.

Carrie spoke up. "Hawkins certainly is not innocent.

How about the double use of his name? He had to know about that. Besides, why was he in that train for the return trip if it wasn't to fool folks into thinking the same guy who rode to Van Buren was taking the train back to Springdale?"

Shirley said, "He's not innocent because he just plain *acts* guilty. Why'd he scoot out the back of that store if he wasn't hoping you two wouldn't recognize him? That was acting guilty for sure."

Roger laughed. "Trust Mother to say that. Found our kids out dozens of times because she said they acted guilty, pure and simple."

While they were talking, Henry broke in occasionally to report on what he could see in his rearview mirror.

"Burke is talking to Hawkins through the Ford's front window." About a minute passed. "Now Hawkins is out of the car and the two of them are standing on the sidewalk talking."

Henry shifted in his seat. "Hawkins is showing Burke something from his pocket. Driver's license, maybe."

"Hawkins is reaching in his car for something... he's showing that to Burke. Something small. Looks brass or gold. Maybe it's the same thing he was showing Chandler Wilcox in the store."

Carrie fidgeted, wanting to turn around and look for herself.

"Now Burke is getting in the police car. Okay, both of them are getting in their cars. They're driving away. Going past us in a second."

"Heading for the police station?" Carrie suggested.

Henry was opening his mouth to answer when his cell phone rang.

"Yes." Silence. "I understand." Silence. "We have the Booths with us. I'll consult with them." Silence. "Will they page you?" Silence. "Right."

Henry closed his phone.

Carrie couldn't help it. "Well, that was eloquent."

"What?"

"Sorry, Just me being silly. What's up?"

"Burke invited Hawkins to the station for a discussion, as he puts it. The man was cooperative. Burke says he told Hawkins they were just trying to learn if he'd seen or heard anything that day which might help them with a murder case. This Gordon A. Hawkins says he knew nothing about a corpse on the riverbank. Said he only knew the train was held a short time because of some accident."

"Liar, liar, pants on fire."

"Carrie?"

"Sorry again. I guess I'm getting silly because all this duplicate name stuff is getting to me. I just doesn't make sense yet." She shut her eyes and worked on calming her tumbling thoughts. *I can't be of any help if my head is tossing ideas around like popping corn.*

"It's going to get worse," Henry said. "Burke asked if we could come to the station after he has Hawkins in the interrogation room. He wants us to observe their conversation. He thought, since we were on the train and also saw the man on the riverbank, we might spot some types of lies better than he could. But I need to call him back to confirm that we'll come. He's hardly going to arrest us and make us stay. How about you, Roger and Shirley? Are you game to spend more time in Van Buren? It's about 3:00 and we're two hours from home. Do you want to see if Eleanor and Jason can stuff you in with the pots and vases so you can be home in time for supper? I doubt they'll want to stay here."

"Well now, I sure wouldn't mind eating another nice meal at Carol's," Shirley said. "How about you, Roger?"

"Okay by me. Just let me use that cell phone of yours and call Junior to tell him we might not be back 'til late."

"I'll go talk to Eleanor and Jason," Henry said, getting out of the car.

He was back in a couple of minutes with a white sack in his hand. "They're going on. They're interested, but not interested enough to stay, since Eleanor wants to get home in time to unload all her new purchases at the shop before dark. I asked them to leave their antique buttons with me so we could still do the comparison if there's time." He handed the sack to Carrie and she stuffed it in her purse.

"Things okay back at the milking barn?" he asked, as Roger handed him the phone.

"Huh," Roger said. "Junior admitted he'd asked that Tummelton gal and her little boy out from Guilford for a visit. They're coming as soon as she gets off work, and he hopes they'll stay for supper after the evening milking. I reckon he's glad we won't be back."

Shirley laughed. "I've suspected something was going on there. And, after all, he is getting close enough to thirty-five. It's time he found a wife if he's not gonna be a bachelor all his life. Maybe she's the right one at last."

"She's been married before. She's got a kid."

"Well, I know that, Roger Booth. Nothing wrong with a ready-made four-year-old grandbaby, or that a woman in her thirties has been caught before by another man. Junior's been awful picky about women, so she must be special if she got his attention."

"Seems we both raised sons who are slow at settling down with a wife," Carrie said. "I now have hopes that Rob and Catherine will eventually marry if they can figure out who's willing to change location. They're both doing well in their professions where they are, so, who knows?"

Shirley said, "Hmm, be nice to have those two closer to you, especially if little ones come along. And, since Catherine is Henry's half-sister, them getting together would make another nice family link."

Henry held up a hand. "Shhh, you two. I'm phoning Burke."

For a moment Carrie was embarrassed because she and Shirley had been indulging in chatter having nothing to do with helping identify a killer. But then she realized her mind had cleared, and she now was ready to pay attention to the interrogation of Gordon Alan Hawkins. There was, it seemed, a benefit to girl talk.

* * *

At the police station they were ushered into a small room by a woman in uniform. The end wall was filled with a picture window, and the officer assured them it

94

held one-way glass. Sgt. Burke and Officer Mendez sat in the adjoining room with their backs to the window. Gordon Hawkins faced it.

"He must know he's being watched," Carrie hissed. "This is just like they show on TV, so he's got to know. And I can't help feeling peculiar myself. From this side it looks like regular glass."

"It's easy for someone being questioned to forget about the glass," Henry said. "Don't worry about it."

"I'm *not* worried, I was merely commenting." Henry glanced at her then, and she heard Roger suppress what might have been a guffaw. She pressed her lips together. So what if Henry had been a policeman for over thirty years? That didn't give him the right to be patronizing. After all, she'd only seen this kind of set-up on television, and watching a murder suspect through what looked like a clear glass window could be unnerving for anyone.

Burke was asking, "Why the one-way trip? Didn't you only ride the train from here to Springdale?"

"I rode the train both ways. Just ask anyone who was in the car with me. That little woman with the curly grey hair? Husband's a big guy, dark hair with white at the sides. You know who they are, I saw you talking to them on the train. They saw me, ask them."

"Some who were in the car say you don't look like the blond man in a blue shirt they rode with from Springdale to Van Buren."

"Who says? The conductor? That little grey-haired lady? Other passengers? I doubt it since I *was* there, coming and going. Just check your passenger list. Your officer took my name down going back, and I'm sure the folks in Springdale will agree I bought a round-trip ticket in their office on the Wednesday before that trip. And say, I thought you just wanted to ask me about who I saw on the train, something to do with a murder case of yours."

"That's right. Now, Mr. Hawkins, would you please spell your complete name for me?"

"*What?*"

"Just spell it, please."

"Of all the... you saw it on my driver's license. It's not a difficult name."

"I want to be sure I get it right, so indulge me. Spell your name."

After a silence, Hawkin's mouth formed the letters slowly, as if he were spitting them in Burke's face. "*G o r d o n   A l a n   H a w k i n s.*"

Burke took a piece of paper from a folder and laid it in front of Hawkins. "Now, would you write that down for me, please?"

"Smart man," Henry murmured.

"He's got him, hasn't he?" Carrie asked. Then both of them went silent as Hawkins spoke again.

"This is the most asinine thing I've ever been asked to do. I'm beginning to think I should have refused to come here."

Burke's tone was placating, almost gentle. "It's a simple thing. All I asked was that you write your name. Now, what harm could there be in that? You do it every day, don't you? Charge tickets? Checks? Your signature is on your driver's license, too. Would you indulge me and write it here? I see you have a pen in your pocket."

Hawkins scowled, then pulled out his pen and wrote, ending with an angry jab at the paper as if he were putting a slash mark after his name.

Burke turned the paper around, looked at it, then pulled another paper from his folder. "Interesting. Can you tell me, Mr. Hawkins, why you spelled your middle name *A-l-l-e-n* at the time you bought your ticket, when it's spelled *A-l-a-n* on your driver's license, and that's how you've spelled it here?" He turned both pieces of paper toward Hawkins. "Maybe you'd like to tell me again whether or not you got on that train for the first time in Springdale, or Van Buren."

Roger's whistle was not much more than a swish of air. "Whoee," he said,"I wonder what that fella's gonna say now?"

The answer turned out to be *nothing.* Gordon Alan Hawkins clamped his mouth shut. After a few moments of silence had passed, he stood, and when he spoke again, said he was through with the conversation and would now leave the police station. "I assume," he added, "that you have no legal right to stop me." He took a couple of steps toward the door.

"No, no," the sergeant said soothingly, "I won't detain you... now. But I do need to know where I can find you easily, since the address on your driver's license is no longer valid. Would you give me an address the Kansas City Police Department can verify?"

Hawkins turned to stare at him. "You...." He said no

more.

"*Mister* Hawkins, give me an address please."
Burke's words, indeed his whole demeanor, had turned
to steel. The change was dramatic, and Carrie shivered,
wondering if Hawkins had caught the shift. Were she the
one in trouble, she sure would have.

"I'm staying in Van Buren temporarily," Hawkins
said, speaking so quietly that Carrie had to strain to hear
him.

"Oh, good, good," Burke said, with all the charm of a
pit viper. "The addresses here and in Kansas City, with
phone numbers, please."

Making the words sound like bits of ice hitting a
windowpane, Hawkins gave him the information. Then,
back rigid, he headed toward the door.

Burke's next words, spoken in choppy, short
sentences full of implied threat, stopped him. "Mr.
Hawkins, I assume you will be available at this address
in town for a few days? If there's a change, notify us. You
won't like the results if we have to come looking for you.
Here's my card for your convenience in communicating
any plans. Now, you'll find an officer on guard outside
the door who will escort you to your car."

Hawkins yanked the card out of Burke's hand and
left, slamming the door so hard the wall shook.

"Whoo-ee, I wouldn't want to get on the bad side of
that sergeant," Shirley said. "I wonder if he's married,
and what he's like at home if his wife does something
that doesn't suit him?"

Henry spoke quickly, and very softly. "I admit it's

hard not to carry your job home with you, but it's something you must learn to do if you're going to have any kind of normal life outside the police station. Not all officers manage it. That's why there are so many divorces in police families."

"I'm mighty sorry," Shirley said. "I never meant... I know you as a gentle man, and I never meant...."

He was shaking his head, and looking into the distance in a way Carrie had come to know well, but never fully understood. She thought about changing the subject, then decided bad memories brought into the open were more easily healed. She asked, "Abuse?"

He nodded as, behind him, the door to the room opened silently. "Yes. I've seen otherwise good men struggle with it. You get used to being tough on the job, come to feel it's the way to solve problems. There's often bottled up frustration or even rage, as well. Guys you know are evil are let back out on the street, and...." He turned both palms up and shrugged. "Some can't shut down the rage over that when they get home. And–God forbid–if you kill someone in the line of duty, well, few can understand what that does to you. I killed a child. A murdering child who was going to kill again, but he was only thirteen."

Now it seemed as if a faucet had been turned on and Henry was caught in the flow. "Those aren't the only problems. Sometimes–especially for those whose spouses are in the rougher kind of on-the-street law enforcement–it's hard for the family to handle constant fear their loved one will be hurt or killed. It's not knowing if they'll come home whole after their shift. Maybe it isn't as bad as the military during war time, but there's still imagining...and fear. Some women, especially those with small children, can't handle that. Even a few men whose wives are cops, can't. In my position I had to notify a few wives and one husband over the years that their spouses had been seriously injured or killed." His voice wavered, and he cleared his throat, then shook his head. "Believe me, it wasn't easy.

"Jealousy is another problem when men and women work together closely in law enforcement. Trusting a partner fully is a lot different than being in love with that person, but sometimes it's hard to see the difference if you're a husband or wife looking at the relationship from the outside. That ruins marriages, too."

He quit talking and stared into the now empty interrogation room.

Shirley, looking stricken, said again, "I'm mighty sorry."

The room went silent as Carrie walked to her husband and put her arms around him, hugging him tight, wishing she could make the ghosts he was struggling with go away.

She'd thought of herself as a caring person, tender to a fault over the problems others faced. But she'd known Henry well for almost two years, and they'd never talked about the problems inherent in police work. He'd hidden his feelings well, but she'd never asked, either. Now guilt and sadness seemed almost a physical pain inside her.

I haven't been sensitive to his needs. Maybe it's

selfish of me to believe Henry and I should stop to help the injured person on the side of the road—offer what we can when we're made aware of humans who are hurting, or in danger, or need justice done. Maybe that awakens bad memories for him. I should have realized all this long ago.

I've felt compassion for the soldiers who came home suffering from Vietnam, and now there are the suffering ones from Iraq and Afghanistan. How could I have failed to suspect a similar problem in my own husband?

She'd known about the boy he shot during a convenience store hold-up, and often wondered why he wasn't more grateful he'd saved several lives back then, including his own. The story came out months ago when he explained about his retirement in Kansas City, and why he no longer wanted anything to do with guns. True, it was awful that a drug-crazed teen had died by his hand, but her mind never really grasped what he'd suffered from the trauma of killing a murderer he called "only a child."

Why did I not consider the ugliness possible in all of his homicide work? And why hasn't he chosen to talk out the bad experiences? Do I seem so self-centered he doesn't think I'll want to listen or understand? Or is he trying to shove bad memories underground? Ignore them? That can come back to bite you, like right now. I hope he hasn't done it to spare me. We are joined in life, for better or worse.

She began patting Henry's back, and he tightened his

arms around her in response. Her awareness of their surroundings had faded. She suspected that Henry King and many others, though they obviously hid it well, were too tenderhearted to emerge unscathed from the rougher parts of police work, or the ugliest parts of war.

And, thank God for that, I think. It's something I wouldn't want anyone to be comfortable with.

She was brought back to the present when Roger cleared his throat, and she looked around to see a red-faced Sgt. Burke standing in the room's open doorway, watching her pat her husband's back.

"Ooo-kay, time for a meeting," the sergeant said, all the iciness gone from his voice and manner.

COULD THERE BE TREASURE?

Carrie's first thought was, *How much did the sergeant overhear?*

The second followed immediately. *How will Henry feel? Embarrassed? Humiliated?*

Then, *Why did it all have to come out now, in front of Roger and Shirley, and probably Sergeant Burke? Why?*

She thought of a can of root beer she'd once dropped and, without thinking, opened. Henry had exploded in fizz like that root beer.

Sgt. Burke cleared his throat again. In response she turned and, holding Henry's hand, led the way toward the door. One look at the sergeant's face told her that yes, he had heard.

Everyone seemed wrapped in private thoughts while Burke guided them to the room where they'd met that morning. After the sergeant's short "Have a seat," no one spoke until Carrie–unable to stand the silence–said "Well, you've got him on lying about the one-way trip, and you proved the dead man lied about his name, but...."

"Yeah," Sgt. Burke said, "a big, big but."

Roger's choked snort startled everyone until Burke's word choice soaked in. Then teen-type snickers broke through the uncomfortable silence.

Henry folded his hands on the table and, shoulders hunched, sat staring down at them. Finally he said, "You did a great job on the interrogation. Guess you'll be keeping an eye on Hawkins and Wilcox. Maybe something will break loose."

After a pause he sat up straighter. "I think the four of us have only one bit of information to add. While we were in his shop this afternoon, we discovered that Chandler Wilcox is selling the same type buttons we saw here this morning. Some of his are supposed to be antique, and he's selling those for $8.00 each. Jason and Eleanor bought a few samples. They've headed home, but left their buttons with us. Wilcox also has what he said were new buttons, and Carrie bought a flower bouquet supposedly made from those. Would you like to compare all the buttons now?"

"Sure, why not?" the sergeant said. "But it's dratted frustrating when working on a case comes down to looking at a bunch of children's dress buttons."

While Henry went to the car to retrieve the buttons and beads bouquet, Carrie put the Stack's supposed antiques on top of their white sack on the table, Shirley laid her buttons on a hankie, and Burke put the ones retrieved from the dead man on the plastic sack they'd been found in. After Henry added the button bouquet to the collection, everyone felt and looked in turn, even using the magnifying glass supplied by Sgt. Burke.

Roger, the last one to test the buttons, set Carrie's bouquet back on the table and frowned at it for a moment before he said, "All the buttons bought in that guy's shop, whether he called them old or new, look and feel just like the ones from the plastic sack you took off the dead man. Only Shirley's buttons are different. Can't see a darned bit of difference between any of the others. How about the rest-a you?"

"I agree," Carrie said, and Shirley and Henry nodded their heads.

"And, that's that," the sergeant said, sighing. "All we've got Chandler Wilcox on is lying about his stock, and I bet that's nothing new for him. Otherwise, I haven't a clue what those buttons tell us." He stood, dismissing them. "I have your contact information. You can phone me if anything helpful comes up at your end." He handed out business cards. "So, y'all have a pleasant trip home."

Roger, still seated, glanced at his friends, shifted visibly into what Carrie recognized as his "aw shucks" mode, and said, "Well now, I dunno if you've thought of this yet, but mebbe two of those three fellas mighta been trying to convince the third that they had access to treasure out of a sunk boat down there." He pointed in the direction of the river. "Whadda you think of that? Y'know, with the smoke stack there and all... mebbe buttons might be part of a scam. What if someone said they came off a sunk boat?"

Burke frowned for a moment before he asked, "Why would anyone do that?"

Roger drawled, "Well now, could be the old 'takes money to make money' idea. It would take money to run a salvage operation, especially on the quiet, prob'ly from under water. They coulda wanted the third guy to put in money."

"It would be complicated, wouldn't it?" Burke asked.

"And, after a hundred and fifty years, well, who'd believe there was anything worth finding down there?"

Henry said, "Some things wouldn't deteriorate much. I don't know about ivory buttons, but there might be dishes... some metal stuff, even coins. Especially if their containers were at least partially intact they could still be where the boat sank." He paused, and smiled. "I just thought of something Carrie and I might investigate. Any of you been to the Museum of Transport History in Kansas City?"

They shook their heads and Burke said, "Nope, but I don't see—"

"Well, wait a minute. That museum has all kinds of human-made transportation devices, many of them related to water. I suppose that's because Kansas City is a river town. They have old-time trains of course, stuff like that, but there's the model of a Viking boat, some canoes. Heck, for all I know they show Columbus's little flotilla. I'm sure they have stuff related to steamboat transportation and cargo.

"The Transport Museum is the largest museum in the same area of the city where you say Gordon Hawkins's souvenir shop was located–Museum Square. I admit I never took time to visit any of the attractions there, but I was called to the Square in the mid-90's when four men got into a knife-wielding brawl that threatened tourists and shoppers in the area."

He looked into space for a moment, then said, "I saw a bit of the Transport Museum back then, and always meant to go back for a tour, but never got around to it.

106

Maybe now's the time for a visit. There's a small chance we might get some fresh ideas, especially if the murder has anything to do with salvage from a Civil War boat sunk in the Arkansas River. It's a long shot, but, since at least one Hawkins is from Kansas City, could the idea about how to fake a boat salvage operation come from something learned in that museum?

"Huh," murmured Burke, rubbing a hand across his chin.

"See what I mean?" Roger said. "If you made it seem real enough, you could interest investors in a salvage operation, 'specially if those investors weren't too particular about everything being on the up 'n up."

Henry looked at Carrie, but said to Burke, "My daughter and her family live in Kansas City."

Carrie, feeling a shiver of excitement said, "I think it's time we went to visit Susan."

"Ah, nothing official, you understand," Burke told them.

"Of course," Henry said. Then, followed by the others, he got to his feet. "Say, I noticed Hawkins gave you something besides his driver's license to look at when you were at his car. Could I ask what that was?"

"Sure. A brass belt buckle supposed to be Confederate. Had the initials C.S. on it and, I think, eleven stars. He claimed he'd gone in the shop to try and sell it to the owner, but the man told him it wasn't worth much."

Shirley and Carrie stared at Burke and Shirley said, "Do you think it was truly old?"

"Couldn't tell you that, I don't know anything about antiques."

"Carrie, you see the same Antiques Roadshow program we did?"

"I remember it. If Hawkins's buckle was old, well...earlier this year, one like it was appraised on that program for an auction value of between ten and twelve thousand dollars."

Burke whistled.

"Egggs-ackly," Shirley said. "Made me wish I had the belt buckles Great-grampy took off the *Sarah Anne*, though I don't suppose they were military. Shoot, all I have are these three little bitty buttons worth $8.00 each, tops."

"I'm beginning to get mighty tired of buttons," Roger said. "Let's go back to Carol's and eat our supper, then head fer home."

Burke walked them to the entrance and said, "You've all got my card. Call if you have any new information."

Henry was the last to leave, and, while he was still in the doorway, Burke touched him on the shoulder, then extended his hand. "Be careful now. And, if you happen to talk with any of your old friends in the KCPD, you might see if they have information that could help us here. All I know is what they told me on the phone. No chance to do any digging."

Henry nodded while they shook hands, and Burke continued, "That's just a comment to a friend. Nothing official. But you give me a call when you get back. You've still got my cell phone number? The one on the card is the station."

"Yes, I understand. I'll call. And... thanks."

As they left the police station parking lot, Henry saw a blue Ford pull out of a parking space down the block. But, by the time they arrived at Carol's, that car had disappeared.

KANSAS CITY

During supper Roger said, "Remember those folks who came to fish in the river while we were there? I wonder if Arkansas River fish are okay to eat?"

Shirley's head shot up and she glared at her husband. "Well, I wouldn't eat them, Roger Booth, and that means I don't plan to cook any. Besides, I know what you're thinking. You want to bring the boat you made for the kids down here and fish your way into the center of that island. I just plain don't like your idea."

"Oh, I'd bring Junior with me. You and Antonio can handle the milking for one day, can't you?"

"'Course, but still... Henry, talk some sense into him."

"He's a grown man, Shirley, but my personal advice would be the same as yours."

Roger cocked his head and looked over at Henry, who returned the look and said, "I'll repeat that Sgt. Burke wouldn't be happy to find you on the river. Besides, my friend, are you certain your small boat is safe for two grown men?"

"Sure it is. I've been in the boat with our four kids when they were little. If other folks can fish in the river, I can too, and the sergeant be danged. I have a proper fishing license, so does Junior. Besides, Burke's never seen my truck, and we'd wear overalls and caps."

Henry laughed. "Wait until Carrie and I get back from Kansas City. Then maybe I'll come with you, stand on the bank with my fishing gear, and keep watch."

"Naa, you'd be too obvious."

"Hey, I have a pair of overalls and a very spiffy John Deere cap."

"Well, we'll see," Roger said, scooping up a fork full of mashed potatoes and white gravy. "Say, isn't this meal great? Mother, the cooks here aren't near as good as you, but they're pretty dang good."

Carrie smiled at the bantering exchange, glad to see that Henry's outburst in the police station, while probably not forgotten by anyone, had at least slipped into the background. She poked Henry in the ribs and said, in a stage whisper, "Any bets on whether Roger and Junior will be down here as soon as we leave town?"

Henry, looking sober now, said "Roger, be careful. Don't forget, a man has been killed over this mess—whatever it is. Getting more involved than you already are could be dangerous. My advice is to stay home."

"I will if you and Carrie will."

"We're just going to visit Susan, her husband, and my grandson, Johnny."

"Yeah, sure, and what else?" Roger said, grinning at him before turning all his attention to crust-covered chicken-fried steak.

* * *

Five days later, as they pulled away from Susan and Putt's home and headed for downtown Kansas City, Carrie said, "So, now that you've spent three days with Johnny, how does it feel to be Grandpa?"

"You mean 'Gumpa'. You heard him; Johnny calls me 'Gumpa'."

"Oh, is that what he was saying?" She laughed. "I was

111

pleased that Susan and Putt left him with us when they went to work yesterday. You had time to enjoy being Gumpa."

"I have to admit something," Henry said. "Maybe it's because I never got to be part of Susan's young life, but one day of responsibility for a toddler is enough for me." He glanced over at Carrie as they pulled up to a stop light, and wondered if he sounded like an ogre.

"I know exactly what you mean," she said. "I don't recall that Rob was ever as active as Johnny." After a pause, she went on, "And, it's uncanny how much your grandson looks like you."

"You think so?" seemed the appropriate answer, though he knew as well as she did that the boy was a miniature copy of his grandfather.

She reached over to pat Gumpa's thigh. "You bet. Same shape nose, same dark hair and tan skin, and oh, those beautiful brown eyes! He's just as cute as you are."

Her husband fell silent, as if ignoring her words. *Probably typical male embarrassment over a compliment,* she thought, as she watched bewildering big-city sights pass by their windows.

Henry drove through the crowded streets with obvious confidence and, for a while, it puzzled her. The traffic looked terrifying, and the streets a maze. Then she realized that, as a cop, he had driven these same streets for over thirty years.

Eventually he said, "Okay, now we leave the city center and head mostly east. Next stop, Museum Square and the Museum of Transport History."

"I'm really excited," she said. "I wonder what we'll learn?"

"Something to help Burke, I hope. I know from experience how frustrated he's feeling right now. Murder victim, no clear motive, no clear idea who the killer might be, no clear picture of how, or even where, it happened."

Finally they came to what looked like a small town's central square with uniquely designed buildings all around it, some of them architecturally bizarre, in Carrie's opinion.

Henry pointed. "The Transport Museum is over there, the big building."

She stared. "Good heavens, it looks like a huge medieval... *warehouse*."

"Hmm, maybe, but at least that hints the contents are from a past era."

"Surely they'll have information about steamboat history in that huge place and we can learn something of value for Sgt. Burke. But no matter what, it's going to be fun."

As they headed toward the iron-studded front doors, they passed a couple of souvenir shops, both showing t-shirts and other wares designed to attract tourists.

"Could one of these have been Hawkins's place?" Carrie asked.

"I don't know, there are small shops between museums all around the square."

She surveyed the area. "I see what you mean. I don't suppose it matters where the shop was anyway."

Henry pulled the museum's entrance door open and they stepped inside, immediately facing the replica of a train station ticket counter. "Welcome to transportation as it was in the good old days," the clerk said. "Two senior citizen tickets? Right you are."

Henry handed over the entrance fee, and the clerk continued, "Thank you, sir and madam. Our gift shop is on the right as you enter, snack bar just beyond, restrooms in the back on the left." He gave each of them a museum map, then pulled a cord, and the muted 'toot' of a train whistle sounded. "All aboard," he called, as Carrie suppressed a giggle.

"Whew, this is going to take a while," Henry said when they'd left the ticket area, entered a huge hall, and faced a full-sized train engine complete with coal car. "Shall we look around a bit, or search for a steamboat section first?"

"I want to look in the gift shop first. You can tell a lot about a museum by seeing its gift shop."

* * *

The shop was located behind walls that went only about a third of the distance toward skylights in the ceiling far above them. Henry watched with interest as Carrie began browsing along crowded shelves and counters. She didn't seem fazed by shop clutter, whether in Van Buren or here.

He saw a display of books and went to study the offerings. He was looking in the index of a book about steamboats on western rivers to see if the Arkansas was mentioned when Carrie appeared at his side. "Come see," she said, sounding excited.

In a minute they stood together staring down into a case displaying cards with four tiny ivory-colored buttons sewn on each of them. The case also held hat pins, and jewelry, some of it decorated with buttons. An easel standing by the cards of buttons said "$8.00."

"May I please look at the buttons?" Carrie asked when a clerk appeared.

The woman opened a door on the back of the case, lifted a card of buttons, and laid it on the counter top. Carrie studied it for a minute, then said, "We'll take these. She stood back, leaving Henry to pay while she ripped the stitching loose, freeing the buttons.

When he turned toward her she asked, "What do you think?" and dropped a button into his palm.

He squinted at it. "Looks the same as all we saw in Van Buren, except for Shirley's." He took another button, surveyed it like he had the first, and nodded. "Same."

"Are these buttons old?" Carrie asked the clerk, who was now hovering.

"No. We carry no antiques in the gift shop. All of these items are reproductions of things from cargo once carried on various means of conveyance displayed in the museum. These buttons and the jewelry in the case copy items female passengers either wore or had with them when they traveled by steamboat around a hundred and fifty years ago. We have part of such a steamboat reproduced here in the museum. You'll see it on your tour."

ENCOUNTER

After leaving the gift shop they wandered through all kinds of displays, large and small. Many of them were being enjoyed by children, including an artificial pond with a merry-go-round boat ride on one side. A display of model steam trains running in complicated patterns through an 1890's landscape had attracted children and adults alike.

"Did you have an electric train when you were a kid?" Carrie asked as they watched the passenger train disappear into a tunnel.

"Yeah. Spent hours playing with it. Did you have one?"

"Huh, you forget. I was a *girl*. The nearest I got to a mechanical toy was a fuzzy rabbit that was supposed to hop when I wound him up. He usually fell over sideways after a few hops. Dumb thing. I think my parents were stunned when I asked Santa for wind up trucks and cars one Christmas."

"Did you get them?"

"Nope. Got a book about an orphaned toy car instead... and a doll cradle with a wind-up music box inside. I never asked for a mechanical toy again."

Henry wanted to hug her and say "Never mind, we'll buy an electric train with all the accessories you want to put under our Christmas tree this year." But, because of the crowd around them, he only put an arm across her shoulders and pulled her against his side. She smiled up at him and he grinned back, anticipating what would happen when he took her to a store where electric trains were sold.

Several minutes later she tapped her finger on a glass display case and said, "Now there's something I did have: clamp-on steel roller skates. I guess you could call those a kind of historic transportation, though it doesn't seem all that long ago to me. You used a key to tighten the skate clamps on your shoe soles. I went click-clack over the expansion seams in sidewalks around our block so many times it's a wonder they weren't chipped.

"Maybe they were."

"Nope, I checked a few years back when I visited our old neighborhood in Tulsa. Same sidewalks, but you couldn't tell I'd ever been there."

This time he squeezed her hand.

They passed examples of boat transportation from ancient history until the 1860's, and finally arrived at the steamboat display. After walking up a ramp, they looked down on the front deck portion of a full-sized steamboat replica.

"Good gosh, it's a wonder there was space for people on those boats. Look at all the crates and bales of goods. Wonder what's supposed to be in them?"

Henry read from a legend attached to the railing surrounding their elevated platform. "Steamboats like the one you see below you were an important means of product distribution to western river-front towns before trains reached those remote areas. Steamboats carried all types of goods, many similar to what you'd find in department and building supply stores today. Everything from tools to hardware and farm equipment; from cooking supplies and dishes to piece goods and sewing supplies came in by boat. Even toys that couldn't be made at home were shipped on steamboats, and children probably helped feed the excited cry, 'Steamboat a-comin'.'"

Carrie shut her eyes. "You know, I can almost picture that. I remember the song about the Wells Fargo wagon comin' in *The Music Man*. We've lost some excitement, haven't we? No one ever sings about UPS trucks."

"'UPS comin' doesn't exactly have a musical ring about it .'"

"True Henry, too true. No more transportation magic."

"I guess nostalgia is one reason this museum is popular. Look at all the people here."

"Uh-huh. But have we learned anything that can help Burke?"

"Except for the fact that steamboats once carried almost any merchandise imaginable, and we've found a possible source for the Van Buren buttons, no."

"If Chandler Wilcox bought a bunch of button cards here, even at retail, he would make good money selling them in Van Buren for $8.00 per button. And, if Hawkins had a shop near here, he must have seen the buttons."

They left the steamboat-viewing platform and wandered through more displays for some time, letting pointing and exclamations replace conversation.

Finally Henry said, "We've seen nothing to really

discount Roger's initial idea that a scam relating to boat salvage was going on. In fact, with this museum as a teaching tool, it would be easy to promote such a fraud because of the Arkansas River's steamboating history. The only danger would be that the chosen sucker might visit here and, after seeing buttons or something else he was shown in Van Buren, became suspicious.

"That rules out Gordon Hawkins in the sucker role, and maybe whoever his look-alike was. I do think we can assume a family relationship there. Our Gordon Hawkins, and probably the look-alike, would know this museum. You couldn't put a steamboat fraud over on them. That has to make both of them, or at least one or the other, a perpetrator. Then, especially if they were related, I think it's unlikely Gordon killed his look-alike. I admit I'm stumped as to whether bilking a sucker out of investment money was really what set off the Van Buren murder. I don't think someone sophisticated enough to devise such a complicated scheme would also be dumb enough to leave a body on the bank where it would be easily found–assuming he or she had a boat and a whole river to hide the body in."

"Might time have been a problem for the killer?"

"Could be."

Carrie said, "You've taught me peculiar things happen in the criminal world, especially when a murder isn't premeditated."

"That's right."

Carrie's initial excitement over the possibility of discovering something in the transportation museum to help solve the murder was beginning to fade. She sighed and said, "We don't have enough information yet to put together a plausible story. I do think we need to spend more time looking around here and thinking before we head for home. But first, I'm going to visit the Ladies'."

"I'd like to spend more time here, too. I'll sit on a bench and watch the kids riding in those little boats on the far side of the pond. Join me when you're through."

"Watching too much of that merry-go-round and around would put me to sleep. And there's the splash of the water. Ve-ry soporific. Don't you fall off the bench, now."

He laughed. "I'll try hard not to fall asleep. The kids' shrieks ought to help."

* * *

There was no one else in the restroom but, as Carrie began washing her hands, she heard the door open and glanced in the mirror to see the clerk who'd helped them in the gift shop. Instead of going into a booth, the woman bent, looking along the floor, and Carrie wondered if she'd lost something. After standing erect the clerk hesitated a moment, then headed toward the basins as if she, too, were going to wash her hands.

Carrie looked over at her, smiling in recognition. The woman was attractive. Blond hair, color probably artificial, about forty, sturdy looking and taller than Carrie's 5'2" (but then, most every adult was these days). The woman did not return her smile.

Instead she said, "Stay away from Gordon."

"What?"

"You know what I mean. You and the police are harassing Gordon."

"Well, for goodness' sake, I had nothing to do with... *who are you?*"

Instead of answering her question, the woman said, "You reported him to the police."

"I did no such thing. I saw him on the train and again on TV. That was simply observation."

"He says you've been to police headquarters in Van Buren at least a couple of times."

Carrie was beginning to feel a little testy. "So what? I had the great misfortune to discover a dead man on the bank of the Arkansas River. That man *just happened* to resemble your Gordon. But lady, right this minute I need to know who you are, why you're concerned with this, and how you know I'm involved."

"Gordon Hawkins is my husband. He took cell phone pictures of you and the people you were with in Van Buren and sent them to me. When he learned the Van Buren police knew about our gift shop in the square here, and then saw on the Internet that your husband was a former Kansas City cop, he thought you two might make a connection between him and the Transport History Museum area."

"Good grief, he went to a lot of trouble."

A dart of worry began poking at Carrie, and she decided she'd better be more careful about what she said.

"Have you ever been suspected of murder?" The woman's words rasped with anger.

"No."

"Well, sister, you wouldn't like it, and Gordon sure doesn't. He says you and your gang are the reason the Van Buren police are harassing him."

Carrie couldn't help laughing in spite of her wariness. "Gang? For goodness' sake, what a unique way to describe six friends who're senior citizens. Did Gordon also tell you about the two different men on the train and the two spellings of the middle name Alan? Those are what put him under suspicion, not to mention his resemblance to the murdered man, and the fact he took his place on the return train trip. What he himself did is what brought his problems on."

"Two spellings...?" The woman's expression changed from anger to confusion.

Carrie explained.

"Well, I didn't know that.... It sounds peculiar, but it would have been Graham's doing. He always was trouble, *always*. I told Gordon—"

"Graham?"

"Gordon's cousin."

"Ah. Is Graham the dead man's name?"

"I, uh...."

"Well, you bet it sounds peculiar, and of course it aroused interest from the police. Your Gordon sat in for a dead man, who's name was also given as Gordon, on the return trip from Van Buren. Peculiarities like that tend to make the police suspicious when they have a murder to solve."

The woman's distress was obvious. "They don't understand."

"To say the least. So why don't you help with that? Why did your Gordon get on that train in Van Buren? Why is he staying in Van Buren now? Or is he here in Kansas City? *What's going on?*"

"Gordon is a salesman. He's working in Van Buren."

"Selling what?"

"Oh, stuff. Distressed merchandise from bankrupt stores, things like that."

"Well, why on earth hasn't he come forward to identify his cousin's body? When did he find out Graham was dead if he isn't involved? He must have known about it when he took his place on the return trip."

"Gordon didn't know he was dead then, and who knows what he thought was going on? He probably thought he was helping Graham somehow, he always has been stupid that way."

"When Gordon got on that train, Graham was already dead. Doesn't your husband want his cousin's killer punished?"

"I said Gordon didn't know Graham was dead when he got on the train."

"Well, what's that got to do with now? He should have come forward to identify his cousin as soon as he found out he was dead. And, he had to know from the beginning that his cousin gave the name Gordon when he bought a train ticket in Springdale. For goodness' sake, Graham mis-spelled Gordon's middle name for the register there."

The woman scowled. "Their fathers were brothers who married sisters, so they were double cousins. Both of their mothers liked the name Alan, and both ended up giving it to their sons, though they spelled it different. I guess Graham spelled his own middle name without thinking."

"And what's your name?"

"Danielle."

Danielle sounds familiar? Why? Ah, Sgt. Burke told us the police here gave him the name of Gordon's wife, Danielle, so at least that's true. And if this woman will tell me her real name, then the rest of her story may be true.

"Well Danielle, you must realize this still doesn't make a lot of sense. Can't you tell me more? Why was Graham in Van Buren? Do you know?"

Anger flashed in the woman's eyes. "I don't care if it makes sense. You just stay away from Gordon. That's all I came to say."

Ooops, tone it down, Carrie thought. *No use making her angry. I've got to get her to talk with Henry, he's the one who really knows how to interrogate people.* Aloud, she said, "Will you please come with me and explain this to my husband? If you want to help Gordon, you must tell what's going on, and why Graham masqueraded as Gordon. Don't forget, this is a murder case, and your husband is already involved. The best way out is through the truth."

"But I don't know anything more," the woman hissed. "All I know is that Graham was always odd. He'd sometimes show up at our house with lots of money, sometimes would come and say he was down and out and needed Gordon's help. He never hesitated to come to us for favors. Gordon rarely handed him money, at least he's too smart for that, but he'd let Graham stay with us, and he let him work in our store. I didn't like it, but what could I say? Graham was a charmer and a terrific salesman, I'll give him that. He was very good with customers."

Danielle Hawkins turned away as two women talking about the gift shop jewelry display came in, and without another word, she rushed toward the door.

"Wait," Carrie said. "Do you work here every day? I'd like to talk with you again."

The door swished shut. Carrie got there as quickly as she could, but when she reached the hall, Danielle had disappeared.

* * *

"Cousins, huh?" Henry said, after Carrie finished reporting her conversation with Danielle. "You've learned a lot of helpful things, but I don't like how it happened. That woman could have been carrying a gun."

She scooted over on the bench they shared so she could turn to face him. "I felt wary, but not really frightened. She didn't seem threatening. She probably just took a break from her work in the gift shop and went right back there."

"Still, best to be cautious from now on." He stood. "I need to phone Burke and give him your information so he can get started on learning more about Graham Allen-with-an-e Hawkins. I hope he can locate Gordon in Van Buren and convince him to come identify photographs of

125

his cousin. Since I don't want my conversation with Burke to be overheard, I'll call from the car. You shouldn't be in here alone, so we'll go together."

"There are people all around, Henry, I'll be fine. Besides I want to look in the gift shop and see if Danielle is there. I'm sorry I didn't find out more from her. The key question, 'what's back of all this?' is still unanswered. Maybe I can think of a tactful way to ask better questions. Any suggestions?"

"No, Little Love, and I doubt she'd tell you much more at this time, even assuming she knows more. From what you said, she's not privy to all that's been going on. For now, I don't think either of us should approach her. Since she's an employee here, she'll be easy to find later, if necessary.

"Besides, we can look in the gift shop on our way out to see if she's there. I'll ask Burke if he has any thoughts on what he'd like done about her—assuming she hasn't already told you all she knows. If he'd like me to do more checking at this end I can call people I used to work with here for help with that." He reached out his hand to pull her to her feet. "Shall we go?"

"No, Henry, seriously, I'll be fine. And if I stay inside they'll probably let you come back in without paying again. Just tell them that you need to make a cell phone call from your car. And look all around us. See... families, couples, groups everywhere. It's perfectly safe, and I promise not to wander off alone. I'll stay with the crowds."

"I don't like it. If something illegal weren't going on,

Gordon Hawkins would have been more forthcoming."

"That doesn't mean I'm in danger. When Shirley asked you to talk sense to Roger you reminded her that he was a grown man. Well, my dear, look at me carefully. Do you not see before you a grown woman?"

"Meaning I can't talk sense to you?" He chuckled. "All right, but stay with the crowds. No dark places, no restroom visits. I'll look for you in this area when I come back."

She stood and saluted, "Aye, aye, Captain King."

After giving her hand a squeeze, he headed for the exit.

* * *

As soon as Henry was out of sight, Carrie sat on the bench again, and took out the buttons she'd purchased. She spilled them into her palm and stared at them as if some magical emanation would appear to reveal the how and why of a murder, and tell her what was driving the peculiar actions of Gordon and Graham Hawkins.

Why did the dead man have buttons like these in his pocket?

No answer came.

Why does a gift shop in Van Buren, Arkansas sell buttons like this and call some of them old?

No answer.

But—she could brainstorm, couldn't she?—*maybe I'm making it too hard. Maybe Wilcox sells them simply because his customers like them and he makes a good profit. After all, if he buys buttons here, even at retail and paying tax, he's more than tripling his money. And he may get some kind of bulk discount, too. People who sew probably love these. I find them appealing, and I don't sew.*

She flexed her hand and the buttons wiggled provocatively.

Maybe the dead man bought buttons in Wilcox's shop to give as a gift, and didn't want to carry a paper sack. Maybe he asked if Wilcox had a small plastic bag to put them in and stuck the bag in his pocket. Maybe the person who took his billfold and whatever else, had no interest in buttons, so he left them in the pocket. Maybe it's as simple as that, and we're trying to make a big deal out of it.

I wonder, did Graham Hawkins have a girlfriend or a sister or someone else he might give buttons to? I doubt he was married. Divorced? Surely a wife would have reported him missing. Conceivably, if others didn't hear from him very often, they might not have known he was missing. Danielle didn't mention other family members or a girlfriend. I'll ask her about that the next time I see her.

Hmmmmmm.

Closing her fist on the buttons, Carrie got to her feet and walked toward the pond. There was a skylight above it and the sun was now almost overhead, so she could look at the buttons in bright light. She leaned against the railing separating the museum floor from the large expanse of water and opened her palm.

Someone yanked at her purse and bumped against her. The buttons flew out of her hand, sailing into the water to join hundreds of coins thrown there by museum visitors. Tightening her grip on the purse, Carrie started to turn toward the source of the bump, but a harder bump and fierce lifting motion dumped her up and over the railing, choking off the cry, "Hey, there," as her body flipped, feet over head. She hit the water, sprawling like an Olympic diver who'd failed to complete her last revolution off the high board.

PART OF A TEAM

"I'll start a check on the name Graham Allen Hawkins as soon as we hang up," Sgt. Burke said, "then I'll locate good old Gordon and get him in here to look at photos of the body."

"Anything you want us to do about Danielle Hawkins?"

After a short silence, Burke said, "If it works for you, you might contact your buddies there and see if they have any information on Graham Hawkins, or on Gordon and Danielle that they missed when checking for me. Or, if you'd rather, I can contact them myself. What do you think?"

"I'll call them to get research started as soon as we hang up, then let you know what they find. In any case, I'll talk to you again before we leave Kansas City. If necessary, we'll find a motel and stay another night. I have my cell phone with me at all times and I'd appreciate it if you'd let me know any news from there."

"You've got it," Burke said, "and thanks."

Henry closed his phone and sat in the car, analyzing feelings of both pleasure and doubt. The pleasure part came from being part of a law-enforcement team again, even if it was informal. Burke trusted him to carry through with the Kansas City end of the investigation. Oddly, even though he had achieved a high rank here, and received more than one honor from mayors and others, Burke's trust today pleased him more than anything he remembered during his long career as a police officer. His input was still valued. He had something to contribute.

The doubt came because he knew he needed to share his feelings about this with Carrie and he wasn't sure how... or when. She'd learned a lot about the mechanics of police work. Now she also knew a lot about the fears and the pain. He needed to share the rewards as well–the feelings of pride and accomplishment–especially when someone intent on hurting themselves and others had been stopped.

My outburst at the Van Buren Police Station only exposed more of the bad part. I'm sure, especially after that, she realizes there's been a private corner of my life I haven't shared with her. It's not fair to leave her believing it's mostly bad, even if what I end up saying to her sounds like bragging.

Not for the first time he wondered if he should have retired from the force so quickly after...after he killed that kid in the convenience store. The chief had said back then he needed to be tougher, he'd only been doing what his job required. Everyone agreed his well-placed bullet had been necessary to avoid more bloodshed, more deaths, including his own. His head understood that. But a softness somewhere inside still hadn't been able to face killing a thirteen-year-old boy.

Maybe spending more time around fellow officers, including those who, like him, had killed in the line of duty, would have mellowed the pain and confusion, and brought him comfortably back into his team.

Others had made it through, though of course, no

one ever knew what they were feeling inside. Maybe if he'd stayed, he could have made it through, too. His explosion in Van Buren proved that the people giving advice–which angered him back then–were right. Running away was no answer. Until Van Buren, his feelings had remained a knot inside his heart and head.

Now he felt a cleansing, partly because, though he'd been horrified when he learned Burke overheard his outburst, he now saw that the man understood, and still respected him. There had been no pity.

Had Carrie felt pity? He didn't think so, but couldn't answer the question with any peace-giving certainty. He would talk with her about it some day.

Henry came back to Burke's request and his assigned duty for the team. He opened his phone and punched in a number he still knew by heart.

"Kansas City Police Department," the answering voice said.

* * *

When he walked back into the building, the gift shop was jammed with clusters of chattering people, some of whom he remembered noticing in the museum area. A woman he'd never seen before was at the counter and she hurried out to meet him.

"Aren't you the man who was with that little lady with the grey curls and the 'Mom for President' sweatshirt?"

A chill hit Henry as he resisted the urge to run toward Carrie before he'd heard what the woman had to say. "Yes, she's my wife. What—"

"She insists she's okay, but there has been a peculiar, uh, *incident,* and we're wondering if we should call the police. She says...."

But Henry was already headed out of the gift shop.

Dear God, let her be safe. Don't let her be hurt.

Carrie was sitting on the bench where he'd left her, but the scene had changed drastically. She was wrapped in a man's winter coat, talking vehemently to the coat's probable owner, who sat on the bench beside her. Her curls, dripping water, hung limply around her face as someone from the museum staff dabbed at them with a handful of paper towels. There was a puddle on the floor under the bench, and another museum worker mopped water by the guard rail next to the boat pond. Otherwise, the entire museum area was empty.

Henry didn't know whether to laugh, shout, or cry as he heard his wife more-or-less reading the riot act to the poor man sitting with her. "No," she was saying, "people don't need emergency rooms just for being *wet.*"

She really was all right.

Stay calm, he told himself. *It looks like she's had enough stress. Simply ask, very quietly, what happened. Stay calm.*

"Carrie!" He shoved in next to the man she'd been talking to and grabbed her in his arms, hearing water squish in her soggy clothing as he did. "What happened?"

"You were right, I should have gone to the car with you."

"Never mind that, Little Love, tell me what

happened."

"Someone pushed... just a minute." She stopped to wipe water dripping down her face and neck, and Henry turned to look inquiringly at the man seated next to him.

"I'm Norton Anderson, museum manager. She says someone pushed her over the railing into the pool. It sounds crazy, and I haven't a clue why anyone would do that, but a museum visitor verifies her story. He says he saw a woman with dark hair bump into your wife pretty hard at the railing over there. The next thing this guy knew, she was in the water. He shouted, and the woman hurried away through the people who were already coming to see what was going on. The visitor who saw all this says he was more concerned for your wife's safety than catching anyone. He shouted for help, and jumped in the water to help lift her out. He's in the men's room now, drying his clothes.

"We offered to drive her to an emergency room to be checked for injuries, but she says no. Do you think we should call the police? The water in the pool isn't deep, by the way, and it's pretty clean. She says she didn't swallow any. But, don't you think—"

"Wait," Carrie's voice said behind them. "Let me talk with my husband privately, please. Then we'll decide what to do."

Anderson said, "All right, you two talk. We'll be over there." He beckoned to the workers mopping water, then backed away, murmuring, "Need to call our insurance company... but why would anyone push...?"

As soon as he and the others were out of hearing

range, Carrie said, "What about phoning the police?"

"I just spoke with a guy I know there a couple of minutes ago. I can call him back if we decide it's necessary. Do you have any idea who pushed you?"

"Not a clue. I didn't even know it was a woman. She bumped into me and I thought someone was trying to snatch my purse, so I held onto it and started to turn and see what was going on. The next second I was lifted off the ground and tipped over the railing into the water. The water itself broke my fall, so really, I'm not hurt, just wet. But, see, I still have my purse." She held up something that looked like a soggy sofa pillow with handles, and grinned.

"Could it have been Danielle?"

"Wish I could say I smelled her perfume or something, but no such luck. I think Danielle would be strong enough to dump me without a problem, but didn't you hear Norton Anderson say the man saw a woman with dark hair?"

"Wig?"

"Possible."

"Emergency room?"

"Not on your life. I'm fine. I just need a motel room, a hot shower, a hair dryer, and a change of clothes. And I want a place where I can spread out the contents of my purse."

"I think the museum people will be okay with that if I tell them we do not in any way consider this incident a fault of the museum or its staff. We can even sign papers releasing them from responsibility if they want."

"Sounds good," Carrie said. "And, Henry...."

"What?"

"I think we should tell the manager privately that we're working on a case and ask him about Danielle."

"Okay by me." Henry looked at his soggy wife and couldn't help grinning. She was definitely a part of his team.

He stood and walked over to Norton Anderson and the man who had been blotting Carrie's hair. After Henry's brief explanation of the need for a private conversation, the two men led Carrie and Henry into an office area behind a door labeled "Employees Only." They pulled up chairs in a cleared space, Anderson introduced the second man as Assistant Manager Arnie Wooten, and everyone sat.

Henry began by explaining his former position with the Kansas City Police Department, and said that now he and his wife occasionally assisted police departments in smaller Arkansas towns when their help could be of value in troublesome cases. "That's why we came to the museum today," he said. "Gordon Hawkins, a man who's involved in an Arkansas case we're helping with, is from Kansas City. and used to have a souvenir shop somewhere near here, now closed. The man's wife, Danielle Hawkins, is an employee of yours."

"Sure," Anderson said, "I knew Gordon and Danielle slightly when they had the shop. She came here asking for a job after their business closed a couple of months ago. She never said what happened to the shop or to Gordon, and I just assumed there had been trouble in the marriage, or maybe Gordon had gambled away their money–something like that. I haven't seen him since she came to work for us. Have you, Arnie?"

"No, and she never mentions him."

Henry, thinking there might be good information here, said, "We'd like to know more about them. Maybe you can help."

A RESCUER DISAPPEARS

Carrie, who'd been inspecting one of her shoes, looked up and asked, "Do either of you know if Hawkins, his wife, or a man named Chandler Wilcox ever bought a large quantity of the small dress button replicas from you, either wholesale or retail?"

The question obviously surprised Norton Anderson, but he said. "We don't sell wholesale, and, as for retail, I don't know. Occasionally people, especially those who sew, do buy quite a few at a time, but we don't keep any records. If someone pays the regular price and we have plenty of buttons in stock, there'd be no restriction on the number anyone can buy."

"Are the buttons exclusive with you?"

"I believe so, but the gift shop manager does the buying. She could tell you that."

"Would it surprise you to know that an antiques shop in Van Buren, Arkansas, is selling what I think are the same buttons for $8.00 each? They're not old—we've ascertained that—and they could have been purchased here."

Both men laughed, and Norton Anderson said, "I wonder what would happen if any of that shop's customers saw the buttons we have? They might more than upset with the shop owner."

"Understandably so," Carrie agreed, and looked over at Henry.

He asked, "Do either of you know anything about Gordon Hawkins's activities outside of his store?"

"I don't," the museum manager answered, "though, come to think of it, the police visited there at least two times in the last year or so. Remember, Arnie?"

"Yes, I sure do. I went over to find out why, in case there had been a burglary, or something else we needed to know about. Both times Gordon said it was a false alarm and nothing to concern us."

Henry asked, "When were the police there?"

Arnie Wooten said, "The first time I knew about it was some twelve months ago—does that sound right, Norton? Gordon's cousin was working in the store at the time; I remember that clearly. The police came again this summer and the cousin was there then, too. I wondered if it might have something to do with that cousin. I asked one of the officers what the problem was and he said it was only a routine investigation. What the deuce that means, I don't know."

Henry chuckled, "It means they didn't want to talk about it."

Wooten nodded and changed the subject. "Now, about that emergency room visit. Isn't it time to leave?"

Carrie said, "I don't need an emergency room for being wet. What I do need is a motel room where I can clean up and change clothes."

She glanced at Henry then went on, "We'll probably return here tomorrow. It might be helpful if we can get in quickly and quietly. And we'd like to talk with Danielle Hawkins privately. Will she be at work tomorrow?"

Wooten said, "She will, and we can manage all that. I'll leave instructions with your names at the ticket counter and, if you'll give me a minute, I'll make up a list of motels that aren't too far away. Should I tell Danielle ahead of time that you want to talk with her and it's okay with us?"

Carrie didn't answer, deferring to Henry, and he said, "Yes, go ahead. In this case it would be all right if she has time to be puzzled about what questions we might ask. She may even try to contact her husband. He's supposed to be in Arkansas now, and the police there are keeping an eye on him."

Norton Anderson asked, "Why are they doing that?"

"No one is really sure what's going on at this point, and that's not an evasive answer. They haven't accused him of doing anything illegal, but he is probably involved in activities that caught the attention of the police. They think he can shed some light on an open case of their's.

"I'm going to be talking with the Kansas City police too, and I'll tell them about today's events here. We will, of course, make it clear that no one at the museum is at fault in any way."

Carrie stood, took off the heavy coat, and handed it to Anderson. "Thank you for the loan. I sure felt cold for a while, so it was a big help. Hope it didn't get too wet."

He tossed the coat over a chair. "No problem. Now, about the police: it would be awkward if they came here and our visitors saw them. Can we avoid that?"

Henry said, "I plan to go to the station first thing in the morning. They shouldn't have to come here at all. If they do, I'll ask them to come in casual dress."

"We appreciate that. Good luck with your

investigation. Maybe we'll talk again tomorrow.

He turned to Carrie. "Ms McCrite, since you lost your buttons in the boat pond, I'll leave word at the gift shop counter that you may select another card without charge." He winked at her. "And I'm glad your dunking in the pool didn't cause more harm. You probably understand that we have a more than casual interest in this. Maybe, some day, you can tell us all about it."

He took a deep breath and continued, "Well now, I imagine you're eager to find a motel. I'll get that list for you. Phone them from my office if you like."

Arnie Wooten said, "If you'll excuse me, I want to check on the man who helped get you out of the water."

"Oh golly, that's right," Carrie said. "I'm ashamed to say I'd temporarily forgotten him. I'll come with you while Henry's phoning a motel. I need to thank him again and see if we can do anything for him, maybe replace spoiled clothing or pay for dry cleaning."

"Ur, I think he's in the men's room," Wooten said.

"But, when he comes out...."

Henry, who was following Norton Anderson toward a desk with a phone, stopped walking and turned to her, "Stay here, Carrie. I'm not letting you out of my sight. You're right, we do need to say thanks and offer repayment for anything damaged, but let me find a motel first, then we'll talk to him together."

Carrie felt an initial prickle of resentment at Henry's order, but it was quickly replaced with shame. He had a right to be concerned for her safety after what happened, even though being pushed into the shallow pool was hardly life-threatening.

Which again brought up the question that had been bothering her since she first stuck her head above water. Why on earth had she been dumped into the pool? It was something that–on the surface at least–seemed silly, more like a joke than a serious event. Who had done it? Who was the dark-haired woman?

She stood, obediently waiting for Henry, but, before he came out of the office, Arnie Wooten was back. "I guess that man wasn't too bothered by getting wet. He wasn't in the rest room, and they say upstairs that he left the museum several minutes ago. What's more, none of us got his name."

THE WARNING

Henry shut the motel room door and lifted their wheeled travel bags onto the platform provided. Carrie dropped the handled tote she used as a purse in the bathtub, put her small duffel on the nearest bed, flopped on the second bed, and closed her eyes.

"Nap?" Henry asked.

"I'm trying to decide if hunger trumps exhaustion, and I'm inclined to think hunger is going to win. We missed lunch, and it's three o'clock. Almost time for lupper."

"*Lupper?*"

"Logic, my dear Huggy Bear. If breakfast and lunch together equal brunch, then lunch and supper equal lupper."

"Oh, unhuh," he said, lying down beside her and turning on his side to put an arm across her middle. "Feels like you've dried out."

"Yes, but everything I have on is prickly-stiff." She sighed. "After I relax for a couple of minutes, I'm going to take a shower and put on fresh clothes."

"And then accompany me to lupper?" he asked, speaking very softly.

But she didn't answer.

* * *

When she spoke next, she said, "Yikes, it's nearly four. Time to get moving."

Henry rolled over with his back to her, and this time, he didn't answer.

Carrie said no more, but slid off the bed, got a towel and her purse from the bathroom, spread the towel on the second bed, and upended her tote bag, poking through the contents to see what dunking had done to her possessions. She'd already checked her wallet, which had been zipped into a plastic-lined pocket inside the bag and was only damp on one corner, but her cell phone was probably ruined, and her make-up pouch, while supposedly water-proof, hadn't been completely closed and still had water inside. She went to the basin, emptied out as much water as she could, then added the pouch's contents to the pile on the bed. Well, they'd just have to find a Walgreen's when they went out. She wasn't interested in using lipstick, dental floss, or a travel toothbrush that had been soaked in pool water. Other items could be rinsed off and were okay.

She tossed out a packet of soggy tissues and several folded e-mails she had read briefly at Susan's and meant to reply to later. Then she picked up a plastic zip-top bag with a piece of paper inside and tried to remember where that had come from, until she turned it over and read: "WARNING, Back off Van Buren case. You see how close we are. Next time the contact could be fatal."

"Henry!"

* * *

Carrie's yelp of alarm brought him into instant alertness."What is it?"

She pointed to a plastic sack lying next to the contents of her purse. He slipped into his shoes and joined her at the other bed. Reading the note put him instantly into police officer mode.

"Did you touch it?"

"On the corner to turn it over. Otherwise, no."

Guilt rolled through him. "This is my fault."

"What do you mean?"

"If I had just backed off completely, and we'd stayed out of anything to do with this case...."

"Nonsense. I found the body and we chose not to ignore it. Shirley showed us the buttons and suggested the trip to Van Buren. None of us could help being involved. We did what we needed to do. Neither you nor I would have left it alone when we had a way to offer help. It might have been tempting to do so, but we couldn't ignore a dead body."

"Maybe not, but I was wrong to elevate it to this level by suggesting our trip to Kansas City. I guess I was duped into thinking we were dealing with a fairly straightforward case of bilking suckers as Roger suggested. Now it looks like much more than that. We've jumped into the middle of a hornet's next. We, and—by our contact with them—others we care about, may be in danger."

"Do you think we should warn Susan?"

"No, no more contact with her. I don't want anyone who's involved in this business," he pointed to the note, "to have the slightest reason to be interested in Putney, Susan, or Johnny Williams. Susan and Putt think we headed for home after our morning visit to the museum. For now, there's no reason for them to know anything more.

"I'm going to phone Burke, bring him up to speed, and make sure Gordon is still in Van Buren. Then I'll phone the police here. Maybe we need to see them this evening rather than wait for morning."

She nodded and began stripping off her clothing while he went to the phone on the nightstand. He was still waiting to be put through to his contact at the KCPD when he heard her turn on the shower.

When she came out, toweling her hair, he said, "Burke says Gordon's still there, and the captain I've been talking with here thinks it's best for us to come to the station in the morning as originally planned. I asked him to check on the police visits to the Hawkins's business in the meantime. So now we might as well find something to eat, maybe watch TV or read for a while, and turn in early."

"Do you think *they* know where we are right now? Is it even safe to go out to dinner?"

He sat on the edge of the bed and pulled her down next to him. "That's a constant worry from now on," he said, "but I honestly think the threat was more to frighten us away than any intent to do actual harm. They'll probably assume they accomplished that unless they follow us to the police station tomorrow. We'll stay alert though, stay in lighted areas, and stay together. My friend at the department, Captain Doug Boinevich, said he'd ask patrols to cruise through the parking lot here every so often. I gave him our car's license number and description, our room number, and our location in the building."

146

"How about staying here and phoning for pizza delivery?"

"Good idea. I'll call while you put on a robe. There's a card from Pizza Hut on the desk."

She nodded and smiled, but Henry knew his wife well enough to notice the cloud of worry shading her face in spite of the smile.

WHO'S IN DANGER?

As they drove out of the motel parking lot the next morning, Henry said, "All quiet and peaceful, thank God."

"Indeed. I've sure been praying.

"It's possible the note was only bluster, or else they're waiting to see if it scared us off."

"I don't intend to stop praying."

They rode in silence for a while, then Carrie asked, "We're going to the building where you worked, aren't we?"

"Yes. At least I worked out of there during my last few years with the department."

"Will we see your office?"

Henry looked over at her when a red light stopped them. The question amused and touched him, but in spite of his words about the note being bluster, a concern over its possible implications still hung in his mind and he didn't smile. "Can see it if you want to. Probably changed, though. Been others in there since I left. They may even have painted it." Now the hint of a chuckle did escape.

He glanced in the rear-view mirror one more time as the light changed to green. No evidence of a tail, but, in this traffic, he couldn't really tell. Early morning traffic was always heavy in the central city. He wanted to bang the wheel in frustration, but, with Carrie beside him, didn't dare. He hoped she had no idea how worried he was.

* * *

In the lobby of police headquarters a uniformed officer greeted them from behind thick glass. Henry gave the man their names and the name of the officer they had an appointment with. Not long after the x-ray machine and metal detector had approved their presence, Captain Doug Boinevich appeared and greeted Henry warmly.

Carrie, who'd been busy trying to absorb all that was happening, turned her attention to the tough-looking stocky man, who was probably only a few years younger than they were. Henry introduced her, and the captain, speaking in what Carrie always thought of as a male-only foreign language called *Bull*, said he was honored to meet anyone who would put up with Major King. "Especially," he added, someone as pretty as you are."

Carrie forced out the obligatory grin and the comment that yes, Henry was really hard to put up with, but she was managing quite well, thank you very much.

Then the two men shook hands a second time, talking heartily about the need to get together and catch up. As they talked, both of them moved to grip each other on their upper arms. Carrie figured that was the only display of affection allowed to males in this location and situation.

After the captain led them through doors into the heart of the police station, Carrie's head buzzed from the effort to understand Henry's life here. Were these men once close friends, or simply friendly colleagues? Had they gone out together after work to unwind? Had they shared confidences and, God forbid, horrible experiences? Did this man understand why Henry chose early retirement, or had he maybe concealed critical feelings? She also wondered how Henry felt about returning to a building that would obviously be full of memories.

They went up in a dusty-smelling elevator, and out into a long hall. Walking beside Henry, the captain began talking about people they knew. He took very large steps, and Carrie had to trot to keep up. Her leather-soled shoes clicked on the bare floor. She felt like she'd been forgotten as a person and was now only background rhythm for the rapid conversation of the two men.

She finally gave up trying to understand what they were saying, thought *Bull,* grinned to herself, and paid more attention to her surroundings. Smell? Older building, cleaning chemicals, and, no matter how many women worked here, a male smell. Not sweaty, exactly, but "used."

Plain halls, plain rooms opening off the halls. Business-like decor, a bit past prime, and certainly not intended to impress anyone. Men and women in uniform and street clothing, talking, bending over paperwork or a computer, hurrying in the halls. One man in uniform saluted the captain. Was that like a military salute, or only a joking gesture? Otherwise, everyone seemed to be taking whatever they were doing very seriously. *Protect and Serve.*

The captain's office was cramped, but included a desk and desk chair, three visitor's chairs rather too close together, and a file cabinet. "Coffee?" Boinevich gestured to his own cup. Carrie and Henry shook their heads.

"Now, what's the story?" the captain asked as he dropped into his desk chair and they settled into visitor's chairs, sitting elbow-to-elbow.

Henry took the handkerchief-wrapped plastic sack with its note out of his jacket pocket and unwrapped it on the desk top.

The captain bent over, read, and looked up. "We'll get started checking this for fingerprints and anything else it might reveal," he said, "then you can tell me the story from the beginning." He took a form and manila envelope from his file cabinet, wrote on the form for a minute, slipped the flap of the envelope under the bag and deftly scooped it in without touching it, added the form, and picked up his phone.

"Duncan? Good. I have some evidence here that needs checking. Could you please come pick it up? I'm interviewing people in my office right now."

That taken care of, he leaned back in his swivel chair and said, "Okay, how about from the beginning."

Henry nodded toward Carrie. "As I said yesterday, my wife and I occasionally investigate peculiarities for small town police departments in Arkansas. Even before this became a case, she was noticing peculiarities. She can tell you the story better than I can."

Carrie, though pleased by Henry's trust, was afraid she'd sound like a chatty amateur. She began slowly, sorting ideas as she went. "This past summer, Henry and

I took an excursion ride on the historic train running from Springdale to Van Buren, Arkansas. The two men sitting in front of us on the train caught my attention because...."

A young woman in a police uniform knocked on the door frame, and, after a few words of instruction from the captain, took the envelope away. He then nodded for Carrie to continue.

"Several things about the way those two men acted didn't fit with what I would consider normal activity for tourists enjoying an excursion train ride." As she continued, she could tell the captain was paying attention. When she got to the part about finding the body, he held up a hand.

"Wait. I want to see if Detective Art Carter is in the building. I'd like him to hear this story."

While they waited, Boinevich asked questions. "Did both of you see the man in black's face while you were on the train?" ("Yes.") "But not the man in blue's face?" ("No, but we did later. We'll get to that part.") "Did either man leave his seat during the ride?" ("No.") "Did anyone stop to talk with either of them at any time?" ("Not during the ride. We can't be sure about before or after.")

After the detective came and, in a few words from Captain Boinevich, had been given highlights, Carrie continued. She mentioned walking down "antiques row" toward the mural, which led to the discovery of the body with the buttons in its pocket, and the beginning of their interaction with the Van Buren police.

The detective interrupted, "Buttons? That's nuts. And I'll just bet you went shopping along the way... right? Women can't resist a chance to shop."

Carrie bit her lip. She glanced at the detective in silence for a moment, noticing his crisp slacks and shirt, his polished shoes. Well now, who shopped for those? Then, resisting a temptation to ask him that, she went on to explain what the television show revealed about the two men in blue shirts, told the story of the return trip to Van Buren, the discovery of the misspelled name and more buttons, the decision to make a trip to Kansas City, with results they knew about.

"However," she finished, "when one of the museum managers went to check on the man who had helped me out of the pool, he'd disappeared, leaving no name or address. That, we thought, was the end of it, until I found the note in my purse."

The detective brushed a hand over his thick dark hair, and asked, "Do you remember anyone being close enough to put something in your purse before you were dumped in the pool?

"No, and if the person who left the note didn't expect my purse to get wet before I found it, why would he or she seal it in a plastic bag?"

"So, looks like the note came from either the person who dumped you in, or the man who helped get you out."

"That's what I think."

Everyone sat in silence for a couple of moments before Henry said, "Yesterday I asked for information about Danielle Hawkins, and about the reason officers visited the Hawkins's former souvenir and gift shop. What did you learn?"

Detective Carter, after a nod from the captain, said, "Danielle B. Hawkins is the legal wife of Gordon Alan Hawkins. They're both from Kansas City and have lived here together at ten recorded addresses. They've opened and closed several retail businesses over the seventeen years since their marriage—two pawn shops, a cheap jewelry and gift shop, and, finally, the shop next to the museum. None of those seemed very successful, but they always had enough money to keep up a comfortable, if not luxurious, lifestyle. As to the department visits to their business: we'd heard repeated rumors about a fencing operation there, or at least stolen goods being sold through the store. We checked it out twice. Found nothing either time, just the usual tourist stuff. No suspicious paperwork, no evidence of unaccounted for money, no nothing."

Remembering Arnie Wooten's comments about a cousin working in the shop, Carrie said, "I understand Gordon Hawkins's cousin was there both times you searched."

The detective, who, Carrie thought, epitomized the term tall, dark, and handsome, said "The dead guy? He wasn't there. Only Gordon and Danielle. By the way, we got photos of the cousin from Sgt. Burke in Van Buren last night. There sure is a family resemblance, but there's no record of the cousin in Kansas City. And, if he worked in the shop, there's no record he was ever paid a salary, either."

154

"It may have been cash under the table," Captain Boinevich said, earning such a cold look from the detective that Carrie wondered what the problem was. She decided the detective was a shade pompous, and didn't like people adding their own ideas to his deductions. As he ran a hand over his hair once more, she added another negative. He was way too conscious of his looks.

"You'll probably want to ask the museum folks more about this," Henry said, "because they told us the cousin was there both times when the police came. Either he disappeared from sight before our...your guys got there, or he took Gordon's place during that time. I don't know if either Anderson or Wooten can say with certainty that Graham was actually in the shop at the same time as the police. Maybe they were only reporting impressions. Carrie and I didn't know the circumstances, so we didn't press for more details.

"And, given what we know or suspect now, Danielle may be easily convinced she should talk freely with you, especially since her husband is in Van Buren and can't interfere."

"Yes, we will talk to Danielle and the museum managers," the detective said. "I spoke with Sgt. Burke earlier this morning, and he said Gordon was coming to headquarters there today to identify photos of his cousin. Now, with what you've said, I think we'd like to question him as well. I'll call Burke and ask about that. I hope Hawkins will come back here voluntarily. Otherwise I'll have to go to the prosecutor and begin proceedings to get him here. Since he seems key to an on-going investigation in two cities, I think we can get a prosecutor's subpoena."

"I wonder," Carrie said, thinking aloud, "if Graham used his cousin's business as a front for selling stolen merchandise? What if the items he uh, fenced, were for pre-arranged buyers who met him in the shop?" Surely Gordon and Danielle would have known what was going on, but they may not have been directly involved."

The three men, as if by agreement, stared at the ceiling. Carrie wondered if speculative input from her was considered inappropriate by Carter and Boinevich, then decided she didn't care what they thought as long as she didn't embarrass Henry. And, after all, he had asked her to describe the events that brought them here. How would these guys put it? Ahh, a stake. She had a stake in all this, that was it.

"Maybe theft to order?" Henry said, and Boinevich nodded. "Have you had reports of burglaries that fit the scenario?"

Carrie was watching Art Carter. He shifted in his seat, shook his head slightly, and looked at the floor for a minute before he spoke. "We always have unsolved burglaries, as you know," he said, "but if stuff was valuable enough, it could have been brought in from anywhere in the country...or the world, for that matter."

Captain Boinevich added, "And sometimes owners of stolen items don't report a theft because of the way they obtained whatever was stolen in the first place."

Henry nodded. "Which, extended, suggests that

whoever might have been buying from Graham, or Gordon and Danielle, knew the provenance of what they were paying for. I've seen cases like that. Items are acquired for private enjoyment only. No public record, and the new owner doesn't particularly care how the item was obtained."

Carrie asked, "Do you think Graham might have gotten crosswise with someone else involved in this? Could he have been killed because of that, or because of what he knew? Does that mean Gordon and Danielle may be in danger now? Or does it mean Gordon is a killer? And, how does Gordon impersonating his cousin on the ride back from Van Buren fit with...with anything. So far there are way too many unknowns." She rubbed her forehead, and wondered again if she should have kept her mouth shut. She was a private citizen in the middle of a group of law-enforcement professionals, and probably exposed her ignorance by talking about something she didn't fully understand. Oh, dear. It was so easy to get carried away.

After a long silence, broken only by a tuneless air-whistle from Detective Carter, Henry said, "If fencing or selling stolen big ticket items is really what was going on, then the threat in that note put in your purse should be taken even more seriously and might extend to Gordon and Danielle. What do you think, Doug?"

"If whoever *they* are know you've come here...." The captain turned his coffee cup around on the desk top a couple of times, then said, "We need to pursue this right away." He looked at the detective. "What do you think,

Art? Since one man has already died, possibly as a result of what we're talking about right now, it could be that the Kings, or even the Hawkins, are in some danger."

The detective said, "I agree. Major King, I suggest you and your wife move out of the motel you're in and come here with your luggage. We'll put your car in a secure place, then drive you to a bed and breakfast where we can keep tabs on you for the duration of your stay here, or at least until we find out more about what's going on."

Henry was shaking his head, "I don't think—"

Doug Boinevich interrupted. "Come on, Hank. What would you suggest if our places were reversed? Carter has the right idea."

Hank? Carrie thought, as the room went quiet again. *Oh no, never.* She looked at her Henry. *Had he really been Hank to these guys?*

Henry didn't correct the use of the nick-name, but when the silence had begun to feel awkward, he responded to Boinevich's question. "Okay, whatever you say." He glanced at Carrie. "We appreciate your help."

Carrie, listening to this, felt like she'd dropped into an episode of "Law and Order," but couldn't turn off the television set and make everything bad go away. She shut her eyes, closing out the tension-filled room. *Dear God, we sure need some insight here, not to mention protection for everyone involved.*

MARRIED TO A COP

"Got weapons with you this trip?" Boinevich asked, looking at both of them.

Henry said "No," and Carrie blinked, then hoped she hadn't looked too surprised.

Interesting. This tough-looking cop considered it possible that a sweet (or so Henry said) white-haired granny-aged woman would be carrying *heat*. Could that be considered a victory for feminism? If so, it was not a victory for humanity in general, male or female.

Still....

She stretched a bland expression across her face and shook her head, half-hoping, somewhere in the back of her mind, that the captain assumed she had merely chosen to leave her business-like automatic at home.

"I'll send an officer with you to your motel, just in case. Give me a few minutes and he'll met you in the lobby. I'm sure you know the way there."

"Carrie would like to see my old office. That okay?" Henry asked.

"Sure. Major Clemons has it now. Don't think you knew him, but he's out of the office today anyway."

"I'm headed that way," the detective said. "I'll walk with you."

After more halls and another elevator ride, they stood in the doorway of a corner office not unlike that occupied by Captain Boinevich, though it was, at least, slightly larger. There was a standard desk, file cabinet, and chairs. In addition it held one non-regulation piece of furniture, a very long couch crowded against the side wall.

"Oh, there's your couch," Carrie said, remembering when, shortly after they'd met, Henry felt the need to protect her from a killer by sleeping on the couch in her home. She'd offered him the guest bedroom, but he turned that down, saying "I've slept on the couch in my office many times. This will be fine."

Her thoughts tracked sideways as she remembered that was the night when Henry and FatCat bonded. She wouldn't let the cat sleep on her bed, but FatCat had been welcomed on the couch with Henry, and Carrie–to her immense surprise–had envied her cat.

"Well, I'll be a...." Henry said. "It is my old couch, but it's been re-covered."

"Yup," the detective said. "Now it's a closely guarded right of elevation to major here. You inherit the historic King couch."

Henry looked around. "No new paint, yet."

"In the budget for next spring."

"I'm glad I saw it this way," Carrie said, moving inside and rubbing her fingers over the back of the couch. I wish I'd brought my camera."

"Really?"

"Of course."

Henry got out his cell phone, held it up to take a picture, then winked at her.

"Shall we go?" Art Carter asked. "I'll walk you to the elevator."

A tall, lean man whose salt and pepper hair covered

his head like a skullcap was waiting for them in the lobby. Carrie was astonished when Henry and the man hurried into a bear hug, slapping each other on the back and—except for an easily identified "You old son-of-a-gun"—exchanging unintelligible exclamations.

Evidently some displays of affection were not out of line in this atmosphere after all.

"Meet my bride," Henry said eventually, reaching out toward Carrie. "We've been married almost a year, now. Carrie, this is... well blast it all Ray, I see you've snowed them into making you a deputy chief. Carrie McCrite, Deputy Chief Rayford Duncan. We go way back."

"Pleased to meet you," the deputy chief said, as her small white hand disappeared in his large brown one. "I have a car and driver outside. We'll put your car in storage for now and use mine. I hope you'll forgive me, ma'am, for coming along with you to your motel so Major King and I can catch up on the years since he left Kansas City. I'm mighty pleased to see my friend again. We kind of lost touch after he left." He looked reproachfully at Henry.

Carrie, staring up at a man who was as tall as Henry, but a bit thinner, felt an unaccustomed shyness. She said only "Pleased to meet you, too," then insisted the two men sit together in the back seat so they could talk. She got in front next to a stiff and self-important-looking young man in a crisp uniform. He glanced at her, nodded, then turned his head forward again. Well fine, she wouldn't have to make conversation with him. She could listen to talk coming from the back seat.

161

After family catch-up news, including the discovery of Henry's daughter (for which he gave Carrie credit) and half-sister (crediting Carrie again), then the latest on Duncan's wife, sons, and grandchildren, the men began reminiscing about the past. Carrie learned they had been partners on patrol for a time, that each thought the other had saved his life at least once, and that police work, like the military, demanded discipline she was sure she could never achieve. The word that occurred to her as she listened was *focus.*

Police officers have to learn how to divide their lives into sections, she thought. *Henry was really showing us that when he spoke out back in Van Buren. They must focus on the moment, whether they're home with their families, doing research and paper work, maintaining alertness on patrol, or facing danger to themselves and others. If they're good officers, I guess that ability to focus on the current moment and its needs eventually becomes automatic. Or should,* she thought, thinking of what Henry had said about divorce.

Ray Duncan had been the first person to reach Henry after the convenience store shooting. Following that bit of memory release, the men's voices dropped to a confidential level. Carrie heard little more, but she already knew enough of the circumstances to guess from murmured words that this friend was evidently at least one person in the department totally aware of how shattered Henry had been when he walked over to find a young-looking boy lying dead in front of the store counter. In those first minutes it hadn't mattered to

Henry that–only seconds earlier–the boy had been a drug-crazed killer about to shoot him and other customers. Ironically, Henry had been off duty at the time, though still carrying his gun. He'd stopped at the store to get pop and a sack of chips. "Too bad I wanted that snack," he said, when telling Carrie the story.

"Maybe not," she'd said cautiously. "It sounds like you saved the lives of several people."

There had been no reply.

Finally Duncan's voice lifted enough for Carrie to hear, "Man, Hank, you were frozen on automatic pilot after that, and I just couldn't reach you. Even Rose couldn't."

Rose? Henry had never mentioned someone named Rose.

"It's just great to see you now, and see that the ghosts are gone. They are, aren't they? You look great, and... *married!*" There was a brief whisper, male chuckles, and Duncan's voice was audible again."That's great, just great. Since you never got in touch after leaving here, I kept wondering...."

Henry's murmured words were husky with emotion. "I was a coward, Ray. Tried to forget everything, shut police work, Kansas City, even you, out of my memory. No guts."

"Forget that no guts stuff. I know different."

"Well, as you and all the others warned back then, trying to bury it doesn't work, though eventually, the memories do begin to fade. I built a new life with good things happening, and the friendship of good people,

163

especially Carrie. But then something would come up and it would crash. First of all, a woman important in Carrie's life and mine was murdered, and there I was, thinking like a cop again, with all my baggage."

Henry's voice dropped lower, and Carrie strained to hear what he was saying. Ray remained silent, and, as she picked up snippets of Henry's monologue, Carrie's face grew hotter and hotter.

"Van Buren... friend asked about abuse in police officer's families... everything just exploded....

"Sergeant Burke there... he understood. He really understood, Ray.

"My Kansas City connections... useful... he asked... here we are.

"And you know what, man? I realized I feel proud again."

Carrie was just trying to absorb all this when a voice from the driver's seat startled her.

"Ma'am, can I ask you something?"

Reluctantly, she pulled her attention away from the back seat and looked over at the young officer. "Yes."

"What's it like, being married to a cop? He worked the street at one time, including homicides, didn't he? How did you manage? What was it like? Did he tell you about any bad stuff?"

He still sat as stiffly as before, but now there were worry furrows across his forehead. What could she say? It was obvious her answer was important to him.

After a pause, she said, "I'll do the best I can, but Henry and I have only been married a little over ten

164

months, so I didn't know him when he lived here. Since humans are such variable creatures, I imagine there is no set answer. However, I've realized recently that I would have wanted him to share everything with me, the worst parts as well as the good. Having him do that would be important to both of us."

"You mean that?"

"Yes," she said, thinking maybe she'd figured out where the questions were coming from. The officer wasn't wearing a wedding ring, but there must be a girl behind this.

"Oh, I don't mean he'd have to relive every bit of violence, describe every bloody detail and disgusting human ugliness. But I'd hope he would share as much as he could. I'd encourage that. Get it out in the open. That would help both of us."

"I don't know. My girlfriend... I wish you could talk to her."

"You have plans to be married?"

"Next month. She's so protected, so innocent. She doesn't know what it might be like in the future."

"How long have you dated?"

"Almost a year. I wasn't through training yet when we met."

"She's always known what your profession was to be, then?"

"Yes."

"Have you talked about it any?"

"No, not really."

"You should. With cop shows and all the detailed

news reports on television these days, she might be more aware than you think. In fact, she may be picturing things worse than they would normally be in real life."

"But I don't want to, you know, talk her out of marrying me."

She didn't say what she was thinking, *Better out of it now than after the "I do" part.* Instead, she asked, "Doesn't police work require courage?"

"Well, yeah, I guess so. What that's got to do with...?"

"Young man, respect the woman you're in love with enough to talk this over with her right now. It may take more courage than facing up to a killer, but it's important to both of you and your future together. That's one thing I *have* learned about being married to a law officer, even a former one. Don't let unspoken fears and horrors hide and grow in secret places."

The car pulled over and stopped, and Carrie looked out the window to see their motel. When Ray as well as Henry got out with her, she felt a moment of panic, trying to picture how she'd left the room that morning. Had the housekeeping staff cleaned yet? At least the pool-soaked panties and bra she'd washed out after her shower had dried overnight and were put away. As for the rest... well, the deputy chief was married. There was nothing he hadn't seen.

But she was glad the young officer had been asked to remain with the car and stay alert.

As the motel's automatic doors slid open, a red Toyota rushed past the unmarked police car and disappeared around the corner of the building. It looked like the same kind of car driven by the antiques dealer, Jenni Lively. Watching it, Carrie decided she'd like her next car to be the same shiny red.

THE LUXURIOUS PRISON

Carrie's concern about what the deputy chief might see of her personal belongings disappeared when he chose to wait in the hall outside their room while she and Henry folded and packed. Ray Duncan didn't come inside until time to carry their luggage to the police car, and Carrie decided she was already half in love with a man who showed such sensitivity.

The police car eventually stopped outside a plain, stuccoed wall in an upscale residential section of the city. When they got inside, all was luxury, and Carrie barely concealed her gasp of surprise. The suite Ray ushered them into certainly reeked of luxury. She peeked in the huge bathroom and noticed it held a whirlpool bath in addition to a multi-spray shower. *Well!*

Henry whistled and said, "Ve-ry nice place," as he and Ray lifted wheeled suitcases onto upholstered stands in the bedroom.

"Rose was with me when I took an inspection tour. She said the same thing."

"Excuse me," Carrie said, not very loudly, "who's—?"

"Does it belong to the department?"

"The department doesn't own it, but it's run by one of our officer's families. They live here full-time, and we use their guest rooms when needed. This suite is always kept open for us. For guests like you two, they charge rates no higher than a nice motel. The department picks up the tab for witness protection clients. Part of the owner-officer's job is keeping an eye on the place. When needed, other officers take shifts. Handy arrangement for everyone."

"A minute. Did you start to ask something, Cara?"

"No, I, uh, was just admiring the suite."

"For sure. Say, that's quite a wall around the yard, Ray."

"An extra security measure we added. No surprise entries, and no one can see what's going on inside. We also installed security cameras and an alarm system, and you've probably noticed that the neighborhood has no tall buildings to allow views over the top of the wall."

"Yeah. Looks almost like I saw around some Italian homes years ago, when my first wife's father sent us to Europe for our honeymoon. Walls hid the houses and yards completely."

Carrie asked, "Do they have regular guests here, or would that be a problem for security?"

"Not really, since all their regular guests have a reason for wanting a place like this to stay, and, though they don't always know it, we check them out pretty thoroughly. Reservations at least three days in advance are required. It's a good location for folks like diamond and jewelry salespeople who carry samples. They also host media stars and other celebrities who appreciate privacy as well as security, and are willing to pay for what's offered here. That's where the family makes most of its money. No one in the family ever talks about guests, so other users know nothing of a connection to the police, and just assume it's a secure place for the needs of people like themselves."

Carrie set her duffle in a chair and didn't say what she thought: *It could be called a fancy prison.*

She asked, "Now what? Should Henry and I go back to the museum and talk with Danielle Hawkins?"

Deputy Chief Duncan said, "'Fraid not. We're taking care of that in an official capacity."

"Well what, then?"

"You two can stay here safely while we do more research into what might have been going on in the Hawkins's gift shop. If we learn there's nothing that poses a threat to you, you're free to return to Arkansas, or continue your vacation."

Henry said, "Ray, this is ridiculous. We should have just checked out of the motel and gone home."

"Would you really be comfortable with that, my friend, especially if there's a chance of danger to your wife? Stick with us on this—at least for a day or two.

"Now you folks settle in while I go to the car and check on a couple of things. I'll be back in a few minutes."

As soon as the door shut, Carrie said, "It's like being in a prison. What are we supposed to do all day, watch TV and read magazines?" I can't handle that, and I doubt you can."

"We'll figure something out."

* * *

Henry felt as frustrated as Carrie. He knew the implied threat in the note had to be taken seriously for the time being, but inaction had never suited his personality. That was one reason he'd decided on a law enforcement career in the first place. But for now she was right: they were in a virtual prison. What next?

Carrie pulled out their laptop. "I wonder if there are pictures of stolen goods on the Internet? Seems to me if someone is searching for an important item that was stolen from them, it would make sense to publicize it as widely as possible. These days it might turn up anywhere in the world."

"Yes, but since we have no record of what—if anything—was fenced through the Hawkins's shop, how would seeing stuff someone is looking for make a difference?"

"I don't know, but I can start with the Confederate buckle Gordon had in Van Buren." She laughed. "All right, all right, maybe the Internet is not really a valuable source of information for us right now, but it's better than reading magazines all day. I'm going to see what I can find after I write Eleanor and Shirley and explain about our delayed return home. I also want to be sure FatCat is behaving around the Booth's cats."

"Oh, she'll behave as long as they leave her alone and let her have the sunny spot on the back of their couch." He grinned, picturing the cat, who was part Siamese and, as everyone agreed, a queen among cats.

He watched the computer go through its opening rituals, admiring Carrie's need to do something constructive. After a minute, he went to pull another chair up to the desk.

For a while it seemed most of the stolen items they saw were art objects, many of them paintings. If something about fencing stolen goods opened up here in Kansas City, then this kind of research might help them find a connection to the Hawkins family. Otherwise, they had no idea what to start looking for. Nevertheless, at least they were taking some action. He doubted anyone in the police department had time to conduct such a wide open search and, right now, time was something he and Carrie had more than enough of. Wouldn't hurt to see what kind of stuff was posted.

They were admiring an art museum's missing Winslow Homer painting when there was a knock on the door.

"Okay. Here's my news," Ray Duncan said when Henry opened the door.

"There were no discernible fingerprints on the note or plastic bag. Paper came from a cheap note pad you can buy tons of places. So, the only remaining value the note might have is if we can match the printing to that of a specific person. And, of course we don't know who that person might be yet.

"We've interviewed Danielle, and she admits she's thought for years that her brother-in-law's business connections were *peculiar*, as she puts it. Evidently his income varied widely. Beyond that she insists she knows nothing, and she doesn't think her husband knew much about what she calls Graham's wholesale business either. She does remember that, both times the police came, Cousin Graham got a phone call right before and went out in a hurry, carrying his brief case. Thus far, that's all she's said, but the interviewer believes there's still more information to be had from Danielle Hawkins.

"Gordon Hawkins should be here tomorrow, and we'll see what he has to tell us. We sent an officer to Van Buren to make sure he comes in safely, and Burke says the man acts like he's willing to cooperate, though he didn't give them any new information down there. He did identify the body as his cousin, though."

"Well, negatives give us progress in knowledge," Henry said. "Remember when Captain Norris used to tell us that at least once a day? But I was pretty sure only amateurs would leave fingerprints on that note. Gordon and Danielle Hawkins may be amateurs, but don't you agree someone else isn't?"

The deputy chief nodded. "The thing that really puzzles me is the Van Buren connection. I've never been there, but why Van Buren, Arkansas? Why Graham's trip there masquerading as his cousin? Gordon would have to have already been in Van Buren, ready to take the trip back as himself. Sounds like Graham wanted to conceal his presence in town and Gordon was willing to help, but if that's the case, using the train seems dumb. Why not just drive? Cars are private, and there wouldn't have been any need for a double. "

Carrie said, "The switch on the train does seem peculiar, and I sure hope we find out why they did that. As to why Van Buren? Well, it is well known for a Main Street full of shops selling antiques and art in historic buildings. Most of what we've seen there so far was of moderate value, but who knows what else there might be? And, because he sells buttons we think came from here, Chandler Wilcox—

the black shirt guy—could have some Kansas City connection."

"It might also be a coincidence," Henry said.

"Well yes, it might."

Ray Duncan shook his head. "Enough of that for now. Time to change the subject. My better half says she can't wait to meet you, Carrie. Okay I pick you two up about 6:00 and take you to our house for supper?"

Henry said, "You folks don't need to cook for us. We can eat here. A card on the desk says they'll prepare a simple evening meal if we ask ahead of time."

At the same moment, Carrie said, "That's a lovely offer, but it's too much to ask. Can't we just come for an evening visit?"

"Hey there, Hank," the deputy chief said, "tell this woman how much my wife loves to cook. She used to do meals for our sons and their friends with less than an hour's notice. And, honestly? She's been preparing food for a pot luck at our church tomorrow night, and two huge containers of some good-smelling stuff are already in the basement refrigerator. What the four of us eat won't be missed. I'll knock on your door at 6:00. Casual dress."

And he was gone.

HIDDEN IN SMOKE

Ray Duncan's wife opened the door and immediately greeted Henry with a hug which–Carrie noticed–put her cheek at about the same place on Henry's chest where her own would rest.

"Carrie McCrite, meet my wife, Rose Duncan," Ray Duncan said.

Oh. Rose. Rose Duncan.

Rose wrapped Carrie in a warm hug, whispering in her ear at the same time, "I can see in a minute that you've put happiness back in his life. He sure looked peaked the last time I saw him." Aloud, she said, "I thought we'd eat at our kitchen table, just like the old times. Everything is about ready. You guys go on in the family room while Carrie and I finish putting out the food."

There wasn't much to do. The meal was to be served buffet style, so Carrie took potato salad and cole slaw out of the refrigerator as instructed, and put them on the counter next to a plate of hamburger buns. Rose poured drinks, took the lid off a crock pot, and called the men.

The heavenly smelling mixture in the crock pot turned out to be "Mama's recipe for saucy hamburger." When Carrie commented on all the work Rose must have gone to, she said, "The secret to easy cooking is knowing how to use ordinary things to make something special. I'll give you the recipe. You'll see."

After clean-up, Rose insisted Carrie and Henry tell her all about what brought them together, their wedding, how they got into work as amateur detectives, and the problem they were currently involved in.

"I'm sorry there's trouble," she said during a break for apple dumplings right before they left, "but the good thing is you two came to Kansas City and we got to enjoy a visit."

* * *

As soon as they were back in their suite Carrie said, "I'm tired, but I'd like to unwind a bit before we turn out the lights. If you don't mind, I'd rather not have TV chatter. I still have one mystery novel I haven't read. How about you?"

"There's the whirlpool," Henry said. It's big enough for two. Why don't we try that out?"

So that's what they did.

* * *

"FIRE! FIRE!"

The shouting awakened Henry, and he sat up in bed, listening.

"FIRE!" It was a male voice.

Instantly alert, he jumped out of bed, sniffed the air, then went to the window and saw smoke.

"Carrie!" He turned on a light and reached for the pants he'd hung over a chair the night before.

Behind him, Carrie mumbled "What?" then said, more sharply, "It's three in the morning, Henry. What's wrong? Are you okay?"

"Put on your robe and shoes and grab your purse. I don't know where, but someone is yelling 'fire' and I see smoke outside, though I don't smell any in here yet.

We'll leave the building as quickly as we can, and find out what's going on when we're safely out. I hope someone called the fire department."

The sound of sirens on the freeway almost drowned out his next words, "I wonder why none of the smoke alarms in the building went off?"

* * *

Carrie slid to the edge of the bed and tried to remember where her robe was. Fire? What had Henry said she should do first? Shoes? But, shouldn't she put on a bra? *Fire?* Her head wasn't working...maybe they could go out the window... her purse.... *Dear God.*

As soon as she was able to focus, getting ready took only a minute. She stood behind Henry as he felt the door handle, opened the door a crack, and sniffed. Then he took Carrie's hand and pulled her into the hall. She moved beside him, only barely conscious that other people were in the hall, too. She saw no smoke, and smelled nothing warning of fire. *Odd.*

Before they got outside the siren noise stopped. It was replaced by motors rumbling in the street and men's voices, shouting.

They walked out into clouds of smoke, and, for a while, the whole foggy world tumbled and swirled about her as people in various forms of hasty dress milled around the large courtyard, dodging firemen. Then bed and breakfast workers began herding their guests into a corner, counting heads as each individual or couple arrived. Finally the manager said, "All here, thank goodness, and all safe."

Henry kept his arm around her and, though the inside of her head still felt smudgy, the smoke had begun to fade, and she recognized a famous music performer standing next to her. She ignored him—as did all the other people in their huddle—though billboards about his coming performance were displayed all over town. She figured no one here wanted to breach anyone else's privacy. Thank goodness, no one asked for his autograph. Carrie choked off a giggle, and coughed instead.

Since the air was clearing and lights had been turned on everywhere, she could easily see firefighters leaving the building, some taking off their head gear. They were walking slowly, talking together and looking around. Well, they were calm enough, and by now she felt calm, too. She watched one firefighter walk along the side of the building, looking up at the walls and roof. Then he disappeared around a corner. She figured he wasn't going to find fire anywhere back there. She never had smelled burning wood, and now there was no smoke either.

Another man, headgear still on, shoved past the group at the entry door and strutted toward the gate. She noticed he wore athletic shoes instead of boots. Well, all of the firefighters had undoubtedly been roused out of bed. This guy probably rushed to the fire truck and didn't take time to pull on boots. He sure was in a hurry now—maybe he was going to call in and report there had been no fire. But... the smoke?

She snuggled closer to Henry, and noticed he was

staring at something caught in a hedge against the courtyard wall about halfway toward the back. With his arm still around her, he began moving toward it. A kind of metal canister. *Bomb!*

She jerked backwards, dislodged Henry's arm, and grabbed at the waistband of his pants instead, tugging at him with all her strength. She said "No, no." Thank goodness he stopped moving and stepped back, murmuring "Stay close to me." Taking her hand, he hurried toward one of the firefighters. "I think I know what caused the smoke," he told the man, "and I'm guessing there is no fire. Right?"

The fireman shook his head and, when Henry led him to the metal thing, gave a low whistle. He called to a group of firefighters by the entry gate. That's when Carrie heard the term, "smoke grenade," and Henry got out his cell phone, speaking only a few words before he stuck it back in his pocket.

Feeling now like she was moving inside some weird dream, she let Henry hurry her back toward the building entrance just as rapidly as he had led her out earlier.

When he pushed their door open, all she could manage was a long, wailed, "Ohhh."

She started in toward the horrible mess of dumped possessions, but Henry pulled her back, shut the door, and took out his cell phone again.

* * *

Henry rubbed a hand over his bristly chin. "They were smoke grenades."

"Yep," the officer said. "Maybe thrown over the

wall?"

"Anyone admit to yelling 'Fire'?"

"Nope. That cry from outside is what woke several folks up, including you."

"No witnesses?"

"Not that we've found. We'll interview along the street later this morning."

"Any other rooms tossed, any signs they were entered?"

"Nope. Sure messed up these two rooms, though."

"Right."

The officer pointed to two large oriental vases lying on the floor. "They didn't break anything, not even those vases. Just dumped out the green stuff."

"Breaking vases would make a lot of noise. They couldn't assume everyone had really left the building. And there were firefighters everywhere."

"Firemen would have made a bunch of noise."

"True."

Henry, Carrie, and two police officers sat on folding chairs in the suite's sitting room, contemplating the room's contents.

"Where do smoke grenades, smoke bombs, whatever, come from?" Carrie asked.

Henry reached over to squeeze her hand. "Depends on the form. Military supply or surplus stores, paintball supply stores, construction supplies. They're used mostly for concealment, but in construction they detect leaks in pipes and a few other things."

"In other words, fairly easy to acquire."

"Yes."

"Are you folks sure nothing was stolen? I saw your laptop is still on the desk."

"We're pretty sure nothing is missing," Henry said. "We've looked at the mess carefully several times. Can't be positive until we pick things up."

"Jewelry? Money?"

"I stuffed my watch and billfold in my pockets as we hurried out, and Carrie scooped her jewelry off the night stand into her purse, which she took with her. I left my pocket change, but it's still there."

Silence.

"The investigation team will be here soon."

"I'd bet there won't be any fingerprints but ours and the housekeeping staff's."

"Yeah. Probably not."

"Whoever came in had a key."

"Looks like."

"Those aren't easy to come by."

"Right."

Silence. The younger officer got up and went to the window, looking out into the early light. She didn't touch anything.

The senior officer cleared his throat. "So, uh, you were with the department a long time?"

"Thirty-five years."

"Don't know if I'll make it that long."

"Here's the team," the officer at the window said. "I guess they're giving this top priority. Deputy Chief Duncan is with them."

"What do you have that somebody wants bad enough to go to all this trouble?" Ray Duncan asked–for about the fifth time that morning.

By now Henry knew no answer was expected, but he said, "Whatever it is, I'm sure we don't have it. And," he added as an afterthought, "we didn't before they came, either. Neither of us can find anything missing."

"What about Carrie's jewelry? I know you said it was in her purse, but they wouldn't have known she had it with her when she left the building."

"I heard that," Carrie said from the bedroom, "I do own a few good pieces, but leave them in my safe deposit box most of the time. What I have with me is costume jewelry."

"I'm glad to hear that. I'll tell Rose. She loved the green necklace you had on last night, and it looked pretty grand to me, too."

"Thank you, but I only paid $50.00 for it. Nice for costume jewelry, but not worth all that trouble to steal."

The men were sprawled in two of the suite's comfortable sitting room chairs. They, and Carrie, were the only ones remaining after a morning of police activity.

Following a thorough inspection by the forensics team, Henry and the uniformed cops had lifted mattresses onto beds, slid drawers into place, and returned cushions to chairs. Now Carrie was collecting scattered possessions, deciding what clothing needed to be washed, and re-folding the rest into drawers so the housekeeping staff could come in, remake the beds, and clean the room.

"You're sure there was nothing of possible interest on your computer?"

"It's still here," Carrie said, "and it's certainly portable. What's more, you could easily hide it under a fireman's coat."

"So you think one of the firefighters did this?"

"Well, any of them would have had easy access," Henry said, "at least assuming they had access to a key card, and I suppose they had to check the rooms for a fire source."

"Yes, that's true. So, how about any CD's, flash drives?"

"Nothing missing."

"Anything they might have wanted to download?"

"Nothing of interest there. You saw the contents—a few collected e-mails, e-mail addresses of family and friends, some church information."

"No records of street addresses?"

"No, and only partial names for those whose e-mails we had a record of."

The deputy chief stood. "Well, we'll see if that dried bit of mud they collected tells us anything. Otherwise...."

Henry asked, "You said Gordon Hawkins was to be here later today?"

"Yes."

"Don't you think we should be present when you interview him? We watched his conversation with Sgt. Burke in Van Buren, and I'm pretty sure he knows that. I saw his car as we left the police station that afternoon, so he hung around to check on us. Having us present and visible during your interview might keep him from throwing at least some of his bull... oney at you. He acted pretty prickly while Burke was questioning him, and stopped answering questions when Burke caught him in a lie."

"Being at that interview isn't going to increase your safety, my friend."

"You think we should worry about that now? Heck, Ray, someone got into our room this morning. They had a key. Couldn't get much closer than that. I think if they'd meant to harm us they could have managed it easily. So, a concern for our safety is off the table."

"Whatever you say, buddy." The deputy chief sighed. "Okay. Hawkins is scheduled at 3:00. A car will pick you up around 2:00. In the meantime, get some rest."

As soon as the room door shut, Carrie said, "Sleepy?"

"No. And after that huge breakfast and all the coffee the folks here brought us, I'm what I think is called 'wired' in today's language. I couldn't sleep. How about you?"

"Same. And remember, we did tell Anderson and Wooten we'd come to the museum today, and that I wanted to talk with Danielle. I know the police interviewed her yesterday, but it didn't sound like they got much information. Maybe if I had a friendly conversation with her...? I'm pretty good at getting other women to talk to me."

"Uh-huh."

"Would your officer friends think we were messing things up?"

He pursed his lips. "I thought you said we needed to do laundry."

"Later. We've got a few clean clothes."

Henry looked at his watch. "Well, our museum tour was interrupted, you might say. And if we happen to get into friendly chat with Danielle...."

"If *I* happen to get into a friendly chat with her. Okay, I'll find something for us to wear while you shave. Whoever finishes dressing first calls a taxi."

He saluted. "Got it, Officer McCrite."

Giggling, she headed for the closet.

DANIELLE

When they walked into the museum gift shop, Danielle was at the counter talking to a customer. She glanced up long enough to see them, and Carrie smiled and waved as if greeting a long-time friend. Leaving Henry to look at books, she began browsing through the shelves of souvenirs, finally picking up a mug with a steamboat picture on it and taking it to the counter.

As she handed the mug to Danielle, she said, "It's nice to see you again. I'd like to buy six of these mugs as gifts for friends. Do you have plenty? I'd rather wait until after we finish the museum tour that was interrupted yesterday to pick them up. I'll get another button card and one of those pins made from the buttons too."

Danielle's tone was frosty. "I'll put them aside for you. Norton told me you'd probably be coming back and I should give you a card of buttons so I won't charge you for that."

As Danielle swiped her credit card, Carrie said, "The manager said it was okay with him if I invited you to join me for a break. I'd like to continue our talk."

Carrie looked around to see if Henry had heard her, and thought, *Well, that's just a friendlier way of saying I'd like to question you about this Graham business.*

Her husband was still in the book section, reading, but he glanced up, smiled and nodded, then selected another book. When she turned back toward the counter, Danielle was chewing her lip, frowning. She said, "Norton said you wanted to talk with me. Why? I've got nothing more to say about Graham."

"Well then, we can talk about anything you like. But I'll admit the story of Gordon and Graham in Van Buren intrigues me. Why Graham got your husband to impersonate him is a mystery to me. Maybe it is to you, too."

Carrie looked around to see if any customers were nearby. For the moment, she and Henry were the only people in the shop, so she went on.

"Danielle, I want you to know Henry and I didn't choose to be involved in your husband's life or your's. It only happened because I found Graham's body on the riverbank. The police came and questioned us of course, that's how it began. The most interesting part was when we saw the AETN program filmed on the train the day both Graham and Gordon rode it. We noticed the obvious change from one man to another during that show. You've got to admit it creates a puzzle. So we told the police about it. We didn't mean to make trouble for you or your husband, and I am sorry if we did. If you don't want to talk about any of it now, that's okay. We can just sit and chat about other things while we have a snack–my treat of course."

Danielle smiled, a cat-like grin and said, "Why not?" She called to the second clerk. "Kinley, I need to talk with this lady, and the boss said it was okay. She's a special friend of his. We're going to get a Coke, would you mind taking over?"

After a long, curious look at Carrie, then a nod toward Danielle, Kinley said "Sure thing," and Carrie led the way to a table in a corner of the snack bar area behind the gift shop.

"What would you like?"

"A diet Coke, Mrs... King."

When she brought their drinks to the table, Carrie said, "Please call me Carrie. It's Carrie and Danielle. You have a pretty name and I like saying it."

"Thanks."

This is going to be tough slogging, Carrie thought, and said, "Do you like working in the museum? It's such an interesting place. I'd never been here before yesterday."

"It's okay."

"I guess you already had retail experience. Didn't you once have a shop around here someplace?" Carrie stopped herself from saying anything more, thinking Danielle might wonder where her information had come from.

But there was no reaction, Danielle only nodded. After a moment of silence while they both sipped their drinks, Carrie asked, "Do you and Gordon have children?"

"No."

"Oh, I...." Carrie stopped, not knowing quite what to say next. Then she noticed the frost on Danielle's face had been replaced by sadness.

Finally the woman said, "It just never happened. Gordon insisted we had no time for that, he needed me in our business. We've owned several different shops, and they were usually open seven days a week. She turned both hands palms up and shrugged. "Besides that there was bookkeeping to do, ordering stock—endless chores. The shop had to be our whole life and the time for a family never came. Actually, Gordon stopped... well, for a long time he and I haven't...." She looked around, watching a family with three small children proceed noisily toward a large table. When she turned back toward Carrie, her eyes were wet.

Carrie stayed silent, thinking only, *I'm sorry*, but not wanting to say it aloud.

Eventually Danielle seemed to decide something reciprocal was called for and asked, "How about you? Do you have kids?"

"I have one son, grown now. He lives in Oklahoma, so I don't see him very often."

"Well, at least you *have* a son. Where do you live? Some place in Arkansas, isn't it?"

"Yes. Our home is in a rural area of Northwest Arkansas. We love it in the country."

"I've always lived in Kansas City, but Gordon and I used to talk about moving to a place in the country. I've been tired of this for a long time." She swept her arm in an arc, indicating the building and the busy street outside. "The traffic is awful."

Jumping into the opening, Carrie sighed and said, "Moving to the country takes quite a bit of money up front, let me tell you. If I hadn't found a job right after I moved to Arkansas, I don't know how I could have managed." *And that's really the truth. Until the mess over the theft of Amos's investments was cleared up, things were pretty tight.*

Danielle looked surprised. "But, your husband? He had a good job with the police, didn't he? Doesn't he get a pension?"

"Henry is my second husband. My first husband was killed when we still lived in Tulsa. I moved to Arkansas after that, and was on my own for several years."

Danielle sighed, "Life can be hard. Believe me, I know."

"Yes, and it seems to me you're the one who's really supporting the family now, with your job here. Is Gordon looking for something? I know work is hard to find these days. Are you thinking of opening another shop?"

Danielle took a sip of Coke and lifted her shoulders. "Please God, no more shops. We've had several and we did okay most of the time, but what with things falling apart here, well, we barely made it out of this one."

"Because of Graham Hawkins? Seems to me cousin Graham was nothing but a problem for you two."

"Boy, am I glad to hear you say that, and I wish Gordon could hear you. He just didn't get it, thought Graham hung the moon. Still does."

"I don't suppose Graham left you any money."

Danielle chuckled. "I wish." This time her smile was genuine. "But at least he didn't leave us any debts, or not that I know of. I'm always afraid something to do with good old Graham is going to come back and bite us. Well, like now. Look at all this involvement with the police, and it's because of Graham."

"Because he was killed?"

Danielle made a sound that was half-laugh, half-snort. "Hmpf, that's only part of it. Graham was in the wholesale business, and, knowing him, there was probably something shady to it. I wish he'd never showed up at our door. I always did think he was trouble, but Gordon never would see it. He even let Graham work out of our shop. Do you know the police came there a couple of times to look around? Of course good old Graham was the cause of that. But did he stay for them to talk to? Oh, no. He walked out and left it to us. Thank goodness, they never found a thing wrong."

"You say he was in the wholesale business?"

"Yes. At least that's what he called it."

"Well then, he probably left you some of his merchandise. Maybe...? " Carrie, not wanting to get caught implying Gordon and Danielle should be selling items that were possibly stolen, stopped talking. Danielle, however, finished the thought for her.

"I don't know legal stuff, but I told Gordon his cousin's stock belongs to us now."

"Unless he had a wife and children, of course. Or maybe a brother or sister? "

"Graham was an only child, and he never married. In my opinion he was too self-centered to attract any woman."

"I hope the merchandise you found is worth something."

And I hope she doesn't remember she never actually told me she found anything.

"I say whatever he left in his bedroom or anywhere

else belongs to us now, if for nothing more than to pay back his room and board. He owed us plenty for that, though Gordon never would ask him to pay."

The change in Danielle was marvelous. She had become animated, and not only that, quite friendly, so Carrie felt free to ask more about Graham's business dealings.

"He had merchandise stored in his bedroom? Do you think he had stock somewhere else too?"

"Oh, yes, you betcha I do. I found a key hung on a nail in his bedroom closet. I bet he had a rental storage unit somewhere. I haven't been able to find the place that key opens yet, but when I do, I think there'll be lots of things we can sell for good money. Cousin Graham sometimes got ahold of pretty good stuff."

"You've seen a lot of his merchandise, then?"

Danielle took a drink, put the cup down, looked at it, then raised her eyes to Carrie's, studying her face for a moment before she spoke. "Well, I did buy a few things from him for our shop. I got to look over his wares and pick what I wanted. "

"Really! What did you find?"

"Oh, porcelain and glass figures. Cheap toys. A few pieces of costume jewelry. Stuff like that. Had to be small, we didn't have room for large pieces in the shop, and they couldn't be too expensive."

"I'm sure he sold things to you for a good price."

Another snort-laugh. "Heck no, not until I bargained plenty hard. He wanted way too much at first. Graham got a kick out of bargaining, and I did too, so we had at it, and I usually came out ahead. If I didn't, I told him he could keep his stuff, and that usually brought him around to my offer."

Carrie's laugh was genuine. "I hope your husband realizes what a gem he married. Maybe you could get a job as a buyer for some large department store. You obviously have the eye for it."

"Huh, dream on as to Gordon appreciating anything. But, like you say, I could probably try to get a better job, and I can sure do without Mr. Gordon Hawkins if I want to. Right now, he's nothing but a drag, what with all his 'Graham this' and 'Graham that' and, you know what? I think wonderful Graham was nothing but a two-bit crook. I could never prove anything, but Carrie, I've got a head on my shoulders."

"You sure do, and I admire that. I wish I'd been around when you had some of his merchandise in your shop. It sounds interesting, and I love jewelry."

"Me, too! I don't have any of it on today, but I kept some of his jewelry for myself."

"Good for you. But how are you going to sell the rest of Graham's merchandise if you don't have a shop? Do you have his list of clients?"

"No, but I may find that yet, and Gordon and I already figured out a couple of them who have shops in Van Buren. I sent him there with a car trunk full of stuff to see what he could sell."

"Uh, if you think Graham was into something shady, couldn't dealing with his customers be dangerous?"

"There's nothing shady about the two of us, and as

long as Gordon keeps things aboveboard, just presents merchandise honestly, why would we be in danger?"

"Well, I'd be careful. It would scare me.

"Nah. We're okay."

Suddenly Kinley was at the table. "Danielle, I hate to bother you, but we've got a bus load of tourists just coming in."

"Oh hey, Carrie, gotta go. Thanks for the Coke. This has been fun; I haven't sat down and talked to another woman for years. Let's get together again before you leave Kansas City. Maybe I'll find some jewelry in Graham's remaining stuff and we can go through it together." She giggled, "Except I get first pick. You can always locate me through Norton or Arnie."

Danielle wiggled her fingers in farewell and hurried back to the gift shop, leaving Carrie at war with herself. She hadn't thought about the possible consequences of talking with Danielle alone. Why hadn't she spent more time thinking it through? Now she'd played the part of a friend, and Danielle had responded by confiding in her.

She wished she'd let Henry talk with the woman.

Carrie McCrite, you should have stayed at the B&B and done laundry.

Obviously Henry had agreed she'd probably get more from Danielle Hawkins in a women-only chat. Indeed she had, but now she wished she didn't have to tell Henry about it. Because of his former job, because of his friends here, and because he was one of the most ethical people she'd ever met, he'd undoubtedly pass any information she gave him on to law officers who could ruin Danielle's life or even put her in prison.

Carrie's thoughts swirled between despair and pride. She'd done a good job, the woman had really opened up, so she could be pleased and excited about what she had learned from her. But Carrie didn't believe for a minute that Danielle was a true criminal or that she had anything to do with the murder of Graham Hawkins. She was just caught in a bizarre situation involving her husband and his undoubtedly crooked cousin and, well, she took advantage of the few small benefits that came her way as a side affect of Graham's business dealings.

It did sound like she'd had suspicions about the source of items she'd bought from him. That hadn't stopped her purchases. What she bought must have been fairly cheap though, or it wouldn't have been suitable for the Hawkins's shop, and maybe that meant it was legitimate. Ahh... it could have been a cover for his more shady dealings!

But now, with a search warrant, the police would probably find remnants of Graham's stolen merchandise in the Hawkins's home this very day, and perhaps access to a lot more. Some of it could be valuable. So, did that make Danielle an accessory to theft and murder?

Honestly, Carrie thought, *she doesn't seem like a bad person, and I don't think she's the one who dumped me in the pool and left that note.*

As for anything else—was there some way Carrie could soften the blow of what was about to happen to Danielle Hawkins?

Wishing she didn't feel so sleazy, Carrie threw their

cups in the trash, looked at her watch, and went to find Henry. They'd have to hurry now to make it back to the Bed and Breakfast in time to be ready for the police department car that was picking them up at 2:00.

She stopped moving. They were going for an interview with Danielle's husband, the infamous Gordon. Afterwards, Gordon would talk with his wife, and... *No!*

She found Henry at the counter paying for two books, while a line of other customers waited behind him. Winking, Danielle handed Henry both his package and Carrie's, then leaned over to whisper, "Hope you'll come here again before you head back to Arkansas. I'll look for those things we wanted to see tonight. Come for your unfinished tour tomorrow if you can. I'll let you in, and maybe I'll have found something pretty to show you by then."

Carrie hoped her responding smile looked real.

As soon as they were in the taxi, Henry asked, "Did you have an interesting conversation?"

"Oh, girl stuff, you know," she said.

"But... nothing at all about...?"

She glanced toward the taxi driver, shook her head, and said, "I think I'll do laundry this afternoon while you go to the interview."

That shocked him into frowning silence for the remainder of the trip.

THE INTERVIEW ROOM

As soon as the suite's door shut behind them, Henry said, "What is it, Cara?"

"I...."

"Problems with Danielle?"

"Yes. She was so trusting. She confided in me, and if I tell you what she said, you'll have to repeat it to your buddies and... Henry I don't think she's a criminal, but they'll probably think she is. What do they call it? Circumstantial evidence? She just got caught in the circumstances."

"Does anything she said have a bearing on any case involving the life and death of Graham Hawkins?"

"Well, not his death, but maybe his business dealings."

"And that's causing an ethical problem for you?"

"Exactly."

He sighed. "You know how I'd feel about concealing evidence in an on-going case. And therein lies the problem. Right?"

"Yes, but we can't even be sure his murder had anything to do with his business dealings, can we?"

"Splitting hairs, my love, but let me re-phrase the question. Did you learn something from Danielle that pertains to his business dealings and therefore *might* pertain to his murder? "

"Yes, I guess so."

"You like Danielle?"

"I do."

"And...?"

"Henry, I feel like a sleazeball. I approached her as if I wanted nothing more than a friendly chat, you know? It took a bit of doing, but she opened up, and now she's treating me like her new best friend. If I tell you what she said, that seems to me like betrayal of confidences shared by a friend. I'm sure she never thought what the consequences of talking to me openly might be."

He took her in his arms, and said into her hair, "Cara, I believe every police officer faces this same problem at times. Of course, because the professional connection is usually obvious unless he or she is working under cover, it doesn't happen often, but it does happen. I've arrested, and even testified against, people I learned to like during the progress of an investigation."

"But Henry, she's so... so *guileless.*"

"I understand, Little Love, but you're just going to have to trust me enough to tell me all that was said between you two and allow me to judge how I share or use any part of it."

He held her at arm's length, studied her face for a moment, then said, "Carrie, I know you well enough to understand that you'll eventually suffer more from the consequences of not telling me than you will from telling. And Danielle needn't be punished if she's not involved in any criminal activity."

So she told him.

After she finished, they were both silent for several moments before he said. "Ah, my dear, what you said is helpful, and it gives me an idea about how to approach

Gordon. I don't think Danielle need be involved or that I even have to reveal you talked with her.

"That's wonderful, and so are you!"

He put his arms around her again and she snuggled against him.

"Henry, my dearest love, thank you. I just feel so sorry for her, and yes, I do like her. She can't have been the one who dumped me into that pool."

A knock on the door made them both jump. Henry patted Carrie on the behind and said, "Okay my girl, you go do laundry, and I'll venture out to face the world."

Smiling in spite of her worry, Carrie scurried to the bedroom.

In a minute Henry followed her, shut the door, and whispered, "Carter." He went on into the bathroom, and Carrie sat motionless on the bed while he brushed his teeth. After the toilet flushed he came out, took his sports jacket from the closet, bent to kiss the top of her head, and was gone.

* * *

It looked like a slightly shabby executive boardroom. Captain Doug Boinevich, Detective Art Carter, Henry King, and Gordon Hawkins were seated around a table top that had experienced dripping coffee mugs, rough-edged brief cases, and goodness knew what else. Neither Carter nor Boinevich commented on Carrie's absence, and it had been decided that the detective would open the conversation.

"Mr. Hawkins, thank you for talking with us today. I believe you have now met all those present? Fine. Do you mind if we record this?"

"No, but shouldn't you read me my rights and shouldn't I have a lawyer present?"

"You aren't under arrest and are, as I understand it, here of your own free will to help us investigate the possible illegal business dealings and eventual murder of your cousin, Graham Allen Hawkins. Is that correct?"

"I guess so, but I don't know about anything illegal."

Carter clicked the recorder on, announced the names of those present, the date and time, and the reason they were there.

"Mr. Hawkins, you may, of course, have a lawyer present if you wish, and you may stop the questioning at any time."

"I don't guess I need to pay a lawyer since I haven't done anything wrong." Hawkins crossed his hands on the table and began turning his wedding ring around and around. He tried to smile at all of them, but to Henry it looked more like a grimace.

"First, could you tell us about the nature of your former business in the leased shop space at Museum Square."

Hawkins described, at length, what sounded to Henry like the operation of an ordinary retail shop.

"Was your cousin Graham a business partner?"

"Never."

"But he did sometimes offer you merchandise to sell in your shop?"

"Well yes, a few times. He had some kind of business buying distressed merchandise from stores that had closed. Once he told me he'd bought stuff off a truck that had been in a smash-up. No way I could know where all his stock came from, just that occasionally some of the things he found fit in our shop. It was all legitimate. We paid him a fair wholesale price."

"Did you get invoices, receipts, something like that from him?"

"I'm sure we did. My wife would know. She handled that part of it."

"Did you ever ask to see his purchase invoices for the merchandise he sold to you?"

"Of course not. I had no right to see them. It was none of my business how much profit he made. If I thought I could sell the stuff he offered me at a legitimate mark-up, I bought it from him. That's how it works in retail."

"And you didn't ask to see records of where the items came from?"

"No. I told you he said he bought merchandise from distressed markets, remainders, that kind of thing."

Art Carter looked down at a paper in front of him, then back up at Hawkins. The detective was quiet for a long moment, and Hawkins's wedding ring began whirling even faster. Finally Carter said, "I understand your cousin also sold merchandise to private clients through your shop."

"He'd meet both suppliers and buyers in the back room of the shop; I never meddled in that." Now Gordon Hawkins sounded defensive.

"Didn't you suspect he might be selling stolen

merchandise?"

"Of course not."

After another pause, Carter repeated his question more forcefully. Hawkins shook his head slightly, then said, "There were odd things, maybe, but I didn't see anything illegal."

"Odd things?"

"Oh, nothing specific. Just *feelings*. There were sometimes packages that made me curious. And Graham's customers would just walk straight through to the back. It was like they never saw me or Dani."

"Did you ever ask your cousin about the packages?"

"None of my business."

"Your shop had no back entrance, is that right?"

"Yes... no. It didn't have a back entrance, I mean."

"Didn't you observe some of your cousin's business transactions when you went into the back room of your shop?"

"Never went back when he was using it. He had a right to privacy."

"That so? Why? It was your shop."

Gordon Hawkins merely shrugged.

"Mr. Hawkins, were you afraid of your cousin?"

There was no conviction in the murmured "No."

"Gordon Hawkins, I think you did suspect that your cousin, Graham Hawkins, was selling illegally acquired merchandise from the back room of your shop, and had also sold you illegally acquired items for your own stock, but you never took any action to report this or stop it."

"That's not... no."

"No?"

"He was my cousin. Why wouldn't I trust him?"

"You tell me."

The detective's tone had become increasingly aggressive, and, rather than return the hostility, Gordon Hawkins's voice was becoming quieter and milder.

"I... well, a few times I thought his business transactions were handled in an unusual manner, but I never saw anything illegal happening."

"So you just kept out of it."

"Yes."

Carter glanced at Boinevich, got a nod, and continued, even more sharply. "Officers from the KCPD visited your shop twice during the past year, right?"

"Yes."

"Your cousin was in the shop both days, but left before they came?"

"Yes."

"How did that happen?"

"I think it's because he got phone calls."

"Did you answer the phone?"

"I did once. Danielle did the other time."

"Was the caller a man or a woman?"

"It was a man, I think. The voice was hoarse. Asked for Graham. That's all."

"So you couldn't identify the voice?"

"No. Rough-sounding, hoarse. Danielle said the same thing."

"Isn't it correct that you suspected your cousin was conducting some kind of illegal business from the back of your store, but you took no action? You didn't speak up, even when police officers were right there in your shop asking questions and conducting a search, and Graham was not present. You didn't say anything then because...? Tell me again why you didn't speak up, Mr. Hawkins."

"I told you. I never saw anything illegal taking place, and he was my family, someone I'd known since we played together as boys. Why would I suspect him of doing anything wrong... illegal?" During this statement, Gordon Hawkins's voice rose, then cracked and, after he spoke, he bowed his head.

Captain Boinevich broke in. "I'm sure we all know how distressing this is for you, Mr. Hawkins, and we're sorry for that. But you understand that we are only trying to get to the bottom of several open cases, including the murder of your cousin."

After another pause, the captain waved a hand toward Henry and said, "I believe you've seen Major King before? He was formerly with our department, a veteran of thirty-five years of service. He is now retired, and you are not compelled to talk with him. However, he and his wife are the ones who found your cousin's body when they were vacationing in Van Buren, and they have been supporting the police there in the investigation of that murder. I'm wondering now if Major King wouldn't like to ask you a few questions. Would that be all right?"

Hawkins took out spotless handkerchief, blew his nose, and murmured, "Okay."

Henry began quietly. "Mr. Hawkins, as I think you

know, my wife and I discovered that you rode the excursion train returning from Van Buren to Springdale last July, replacing your cousin who rode down using your name. We learned that as a certainty when we saw photos of both you and your cousin on the television program, 'Exploring Arkansas' earlier this fall. It has since been verified using other sources. So, can you please tell us who planned the switch?"

"Uh, Graham did."

"What reason did he give you?"

"He said he suspected one of his dealers in Van Buren was cheating him out of profits on valuable items he'd consigned there. He wanted to check up on him secretly."

"He said *one* of his dealers?"

"I'm pretty sure."

"And he said *him?*"

"Well, I think he said him."

"But he didn't travel in disguise."

"Didn't need to. As I understood it, he always shipped stuff or worked with couriers, so the folks at this outlet had never seen him. The whole idea was that we looked alike, and no one would know he was in town. It was sort of like working under cover."

"But if no one knew what he looked like...."

"Uh, yeah, I guess... well, I don't know exactly. He had some reason."

"Why didn't he just drive down? Seems simpler."

"I kind of wondered that myself, but he said the only one on record in Van Buren needed to be Gordon

Hawkins, a tourist who wanted to ride the train both ways. I said I'd do it. Why not? He was paying my expenses and more, and Danielle could handle the shop."

"I hate to bring this up, Mr. Hawkins, but did it never occur to you that he might have wanted to use you as a scapegoat if there was trouble of some kind? After all, your name was on the railway passenger records and the motel bill."

Gordon Hawkins stared at Henry blankly for several moments before what had been implied penetrated his thinking. Henry could tell when that happened because the man's bones appeared to lose strength right before his eyes, and he slumped in his chair.

"Help me get this straight. You drove from here to Van Buren, when? A day before the train ride?"

"That's it," Hawkins said, looking at the table top.

"So you and your car were already there on Friday, maybe at a motel?"

"That's right." Hawkins still didn't look at Henry.

"Graham must have come down earlier, because he bought a ticket at the Springdale depot on Wednesday before the Saturday excursion."

"I guess so."

"He left the return ticket somewhere for you?"

"No." He was mumbling again. "He gave it to me in Van Buren. We met there on Saturday morning."

"Could you speak a little louder, please?"

A nod.

"Where did you meet?"

"In my motel room. He said we couldn't be seen in

public together. The motel wasn't too far from the depot. He came there from the train. I gave him my car keys, he gave me his. He left, and I stayed in the motel until nearly train time. I never saw him again. Not alive, I mean, I...."

Hawkins's voice wavered and faded into silence and Henry waited until he had regained control.

"I'm sorry to cause distress. Do you need to rest for a while? We can bring you coffee or pop. Maybe a drink of water? I only have a few more questions."

"I don't want anything to drink. Go ahead." Now the man sounded resigned.

"You told Sergeant Burke you had no idea your cousin had been killed when you boarded the train for the return trip."

"That's right. I didn't know."

"So, you got off the train in Springdale and drove back to Kansas City in Graham's car, still not knowing."

"Yes."

"Then what? When did you learn your cousin was dead?"

"Well, he never came back here with my car, and then someone from Van Buren called."

"And that person was...."

"She gave the name Jenni. Then she told me Graham was dead and she was sorry, and hung up."

"Would that be Jenni Lively, owner of Lively Antiques?"

"Yes, that's what I found out. Jenni Lively."

"So you went to Van Buren to locate her and learn

more about your cousin's death?"

"Yes."

"What did you learn?"

Hawkins cleared his throat and said, "I think I will take that drink of water."

They sat in silence while an officer brought the water, and Henry thought about what Carrie had said, and what the man had told them so far.

After Hawkins emptied the bottle, he looked at the ceiling for a moment, then back at Henry, who repeated, "What did you learn from Jenni Lively?"

"Nothing. Oh, she was real nice and sympathetic, but she couldn't tell me anything about Graham's death. I don't even know how she learned who he was, because all she showed me was an article from their newspaper about an unidentified body found by the river on the same day Graham and I were there. There wasn't a picture, so I don't know how she knew we were related or found me."

"She refused to tell you more?"

"No, not exactly refused. She just kept saying she didn't know, she didn't know, when I asked questions. So I left the shop.

"And that was the end of your contact with her?"

"Yes. Well, at that time it was. Actually she also said my car had been left by her houseboat and she had it in a safe place if I wanted to come back with someone who could drive it home."

"Ah. So she must have gotten your car keys somehow."

"Oh, well, I didn't think, well, Graham could have left them in the car by mistake."

Now the man's brows were furrowed in puzzled concentration.

"She probably found information about you on the registration and insurance papers in your glove box, and that's how she located you."

"Oh, yeah. I guess she could have done that."

"Did you eventually get your car?"

"Yes. I came back here to Kansas City that afternoon. Our shop was closed down by then and Danielle was working at the museum, but she was off the next day, so she went with me and we got the car."

"So you saw Lively again when you got your car keys. Did she give you any more information?"

"No, just gave me the keys and told me where the car was."

"Where was it?"

"In a shed near the river."

"I see. When we're through here, would you please write down a description of how to find that shed?"

Hawkins nodded.

"Have you made contact with other antiques dealers in Van Buren since then?"

"Well...."

Henry broke in. "We know you did. Remember, we saw you in Chandler Wilcox's shop."

"Oh yeah, I do remember. Well, I was just asking people along Main Street, you know... about Graham, I mean."

"Did Wilcox know anything?"

"Said he didn't."

"Seems to me your first step should have been to ask the Van Buren Police about your cousin. Why didn't you do that?"

"I was afraid. I didn't want to get involved in anything that... well, I didn't even know what I was getting into. I didn't understand anything about Graham's connections in Van Buren. I didn't want to be identified with whatever they were."

"Even when you realized the police knew how much the two of you looked alike, and about the substitution on the train?"

"I just thought... I thought if I kept quiet and said nothing it would all go away. No one could prove anything except that Graham and I switched places on the train."

"So you suspected you'd gotten involved in something illegal?"

"I...."

"Didn't you realize you might be under suspicion for your cousin's murder?"

Hawkins gave Henry a startled look, and shook his head, then looked down at his hands. He was no longer turning the wedding ring.

"So you were staying in Van Buren when we saw you."

"Yes. I told you, I wanted to find out more about Graham."

"And you just *happened* to be in Wilcox's shop when

we walked in that day."

"Well yes, I just happened to be there. Why else?"

Henry remembered what Roger had said about mothers knowing by instinct when their children were lying and, because of practice, could sometimes detect others' lies. He thought many police officers had that ability. Whatever... Hawkins was lying.

"Mr. Hawkins, didn't your cousin store some of his merchandise in your home?"

Gordon's twitch rewarded him, and he continued, "I think, in fact, that he left items you were sure you could sell stored in your house, maybe in the room where he slept?"

"Uh...."

"Isn't that where you found some of his merchandise?"

Silence.

"Where did you get the Confederate buckle you were showing Mr. Wilcox when we walked in the store? Were you trying to sell some of Graham's remaining stock to Chandler Wilcox? After all, as you said, your shop was closed. I imagine you needed money. Seems logical that you—"

Gordon Hawkins buried his face in his hands and began sobbing.

Unwilling to quit when some of Carrie's information was beginning to pay off, Henry waited only a minute before he continued,

"Mr. Hawkins, don't you have some of your cousin's merchandise in your car trunk right now, and in your home as well?"

The man nodded, but he didn't look up.

"Would you mind if we looked at those items? If we can check them against lists of stolen property, then we can either clear your cousin, and now you, of possessing and selling stolen goods, or we can prove to you that they were stolen. We could, of course check this through other channels, but it will be so much easier for all of us, including you, if we don't have to. Will you open the trunk of your car for us, then allow us to look at Graham's merchandise in your home? It's the quickest way to get this over with."

Doug Boinevich, Art Carter, and Henry sat very still for a while, listening to Gordon Hawkins's struggle to quiet body-shaking sobs. Finally he wiped his face and looked up at Henry. "Graham bought me the blue shirt as a gift. Said blue was my color and I should wear it on the trip. I saw in Van Buren he had on one just like it. It reminded me that we used to pretend we were twins when we were kids, and I...." He stopped, and looked down at the table again.

Henry reached out to lay his hand on Gordon's arm for a moment before the man went on. "But I really didn't know anything," he said. "Really. I mean, Graham's business dealings were always, well, his own style. I was used to that. I still think he only bought distressed stuff like he said, but you might as well check. I'll be glad to get this over with. We can go to my car now."

WHAT NEXT, DETECTIVE?

"Then what?" Carrie asked, as soon as Henry finished his report on the interview with Gordon Hawkins.

"Smooth as could be. We went to Hawkins's car, he opened the trunk, Carter signed for two boxes that were taken into the building for further inspection. Then we followed Hawkins to his house, removed eight more boxes, signed for those, loaded them into the police van. That was it. Oh, I did find a nail hidden on the inside of Graham's closet door frame. It was empty, but I showed it to the guys, thinking it might have held a key or keys. Hawkins said he didn't know anything about it."

"Ah ha. And what was in the boxes?"

"It wasn't my business to look. Hawkins and Carter opened them together before Carter signed for them, but I saw only a few things. Carter looked through most of the contents by himself while Hawkins and I were checking the rest of the house to make sure Graham hadn't stashed something anywhere else. I did see jewelry in a small box. It looked like nice stuff, probably old, but I wasn't very close so can't say for sure. One box had stacks of embroidered fabric, maybe oriental. I also saw Carter looking at a pair of ivory-handled pistols in a velvet-lined leather case. I think antique guns are an interest of his."

"But you saw no boxes of several things all alike, no patriotic, comedic, or historic figurines in containers divided like egg cartons and packed with foam beads? No mugs, toys, enameled spoons, souvenir plates, scented candles, or—?"

"I know what you're getting at. Was there anything that looked like new merchandise from a bankrupt store or distressed warehousing business? No, not that I saw. Honestly? My bet's on all of it being stolen."

"Well, if what you saw is typical, it should be easy to identify and trace."

"Hope so."

"I don't suppose Danielle came home while you were in her house?"

"She didn't, but I guess we just missed her. Gordon kept saying she ought to be home any minute. I think he was counting on her to give him some spine. When he finally understood that his cousin was probably just using him, his backbone simply collapsed, along with his belief that Graham could do no wrong."

"Are you sorry you had to do that to him?"

"It comes with the territory. The man would have had to face reality sometime. I just brought it about sooner."

She sighed. "Sometimes I do wonder why I got involved in this business."

"You want to bow out?"

"Generally?"

"Well, that too, but I was referring to the Graham Hawkins case."

"It's pretty much over for us, isn't it? What more can we do here? As for the murder, all you have to do is tell Burke what's been learned at this end, and we can be out of that, too, can't we? I've discovered I don't like being caught in a straight-out criminal case like this. Other things we've been involved in have been more personal... smaller, somehow. Before now our investigations were woven into the fiber of what was going on in our lives, for better or for worse. This is different. We're not much more than spectators at the beck and call of police officers."

"I don't see it that way. Your interview with Danielle, for example, was a big step forward, and that was all on your own. Besides, I don't call your getting dumped in that pool, the threatening note, or the fake fire alarm and room search being spectators. We've done something to cause that, though I sure can't figure out what they were looking for in our room. In any case, we're involved up to our ears."

"Hmmm, may be. But if we just walk away...? It's kind of like I'm sitting back of the goal in an arena where a hockey game is being played. A puck comes into the audience at a hundred miles an hour, splitting the empty seat next to me. I'm a spectator in the line of fire. I just happened to be there. Trouble came close, but it didn't cause me any real harm, except maybe a scare. After the game I get up and walk out, no worse for wear. Incident over."

"It's more than that, if you're referring to this case. Think back, Cara. We got involved, and our friends along with us, because we had something to offer. Now there are still way too many unknowns hanging out there."

"I wish I hadn't seen Graham's body."

He sat in silence for a minute, then said, "I'm not so

sure that wasn't a good thing, over all. The man would have been just as dead, no matter who saw his body first. Would you have wanted some kid to find him?"

It was her turn to be quiet. Finally she said, "No, of course not. Forgive me, my love. Without all that's happened since we walked along the river, you wouldn't have understood as much about the value of your life as a police officer, would you? At least not yet. And I wouldn't have understood what a ninny I was not to realize the type of challenges you and your colleagues–past, present, and future–face."

He didn't answer, but when she started to speak again, he held up his hand. Finally he said, "You know when I went out to the car to talk with Burke while you were getting dunked in the pool?"

"Uh-huh."

He looked at the ceiling and pursed his lips. "I never told you about our conversation. Carrie, he respects me. I don't know exactly how I knew, but I did. He talked to me like a partner would. Trusting, you know. He trusted me to carry through on the Kansas City end."

She said nothing, realizing her feelings about the Hawkins case were being forced into a drastic turn-around. There would be no escape until it was over.

He went on, sounding like he was talking to himself. "At first I wasn't sure whether or not he'd heard what I said when... when I threw all those ugly memories out at you guys."

"My love, that's exactly it. You threw them *out*."

"Yes, I guess so, if you mean I quit bottling them up.

216

But Burke did hear me, and he understood. He didn't judge me. I always thought other cops believed I hadn't been tough enough, that I was weak because I retired rather than stay on for a few more years and maybe make deputy chief like Ray did.

"But, by treating me as part of his team, talking with me like I was used to back here in KC, Burke made me proud of my profession again. It was like I was a fresh recruit, starting out full of pride and expectation and a belief I could make the world a better place. I felt valuable again."

Carrie waited, not wanting to spoil this moment.

"What's more, when he called the department here for a background check on me—"

"When he WHAT?"

"Shhh, Cara, that's only good police procedure. He didn't know me, I might have been retired for any number of negative reasons. If he was going to allow me input on this case he had to be sure I was okay.

"Anyway, he said they gave him a report on my service that was full of praise. That was nice to hear, and he seemed impressed."

"Well, I should think so!"

He stopped to give her a tolerant smile before continuing, "What I want to tell you sounds like the opposite of what you've been saying to me just now, and it's this. I have learned to understand and agree with something you've said over and over in the past. When we're given the opportunity to help bring justice and safety and resolution to people, then that's what we need to do. And now it's exactly what I *want* to do. With you. Because we are doing something valuable, even in this case, when it seems to you that we're just at the beck and call of police officers."

He stood, and pulled her up into his arms. "Do you understand?"

She nodded, her face rubbing against the softness of his knit shirt.

"Umm," he said. "You sure smell good. Clean."

"It's all that laundry soap."

"Nope. It's a Carrie smell. And now, Madam, I'd like to smell some food."

"No surprise. I asked about supper here right after you left, and placed an order for this evening. I hope you like my choices." She looked at her watch. "We're due in the dining room in thirty minutes for green salad, beef ragout, chilled fruit compote, and a choice of desserts. That gives me time to check e-mail and see if anything's new with the Stacks or Booths."

"I'll wash up."

When he came out of the bathroom she said, "Well, I don't know whether to be surprised or not. Honestly, it seems kinda funny. Roger and Junior did take their boat down to the Arkansas. They caught a few fish and saw that steamship smokestack–or whatever it is–in the middle of the island. Shirley says Roger and Junior told her it's in very squishy mud like Mendez found. They thought, if it really is a smokestack, it must not be connected to anything down below, because it's leaning enough that the side of any attached steamboat would be

218

at the surface. They took a picture. Here it is."

He looked over her shoulder. "Huh. Interesting. I admit I'd like to get in their little boat and see it for myself."

"Henry King, you surely don't mean that. A photo is enough. I can't believe poking around on a mucky island to see it for yourself will help move the case forward. Besides, this huge piece of metal pipe might not have anything to do with a ship. It could be a culvert, or something like that, washed there in a flood. If it is a smokestack, let Burke deal with it."

He patted her shoulder. "Okay wife, I won't go smokestack hunting. I admit it would just be a sense of adventure that got me in a boat headed inside that island."

"Right. So, what shall I tell Shirley and Roger?"

"Thank them for the picture and tell them... uh, 'Can't wait to get home so we can talk.' That sound okay?"

She laughed. "For a man. Okay, I'll say that... approximately. Be with you in a minute."

On the way to the dining room, he said. "Forgot to tell you. Carter and Boinevich don't know, of course, that you've talked with Danielle. Boinevich wants us to go with Carter to the museum tomorrow morning for a chat with her. Can you handle that?"

"Oh, gosh. Well, I am part of the team, I'll handle it. But let me call the museum to see if she'll be working tomorrow. I need to borrow your cell phone; mine didn't survive its dunking."

He handed the phone to her. "You know their number?"

"Yes, because, except for the prefix, it's the same as our bank's." She dialed, hoping Danielle would be off the next day, but the answering voice said, "Yes, she'll be here in the morning."

Worse luck!

* * *

When they returned to their suite after supper, Henry said, "This is a great place to stay. That meal was wonderful."

He looked around, seeming to notice details for the first time since the room had been returned to full order. "Housekeeping did a great job putting all this back together, didn't they?"

"To say the least. They were still adding a few touches while I was gone to the laundry room this afternoon. The only thing that's missing now are those vases of artificial greenery. They sent them out to have new arrangements made. The head housekeeper said they tried to put the old greenery back in, but couldn't make it look right."

"Really? The vases weren't here at all today?"

She shook her head.

He stood in the middle of the room, frowning. "While Carter and I were driving to the interview with Hawkins, we talked some about this place. He mentioned the luxury, and all the fancy little details, like vases with fake green branches in them. He even made a joke of it, saying they weren't real leaves, they probably got dusty, and he didn't see how dusty leaves added anything to the comfort of the room."

She stared at him. "Huh. That's interesting."

"Yes."

"Well, he's probably seen the suite some other time. Brought people here, or something?"

"Probably."

"Probably."

After a pause he said, "Well, Little Love, I say we forget everything else and spend the rest of the evening making use of the luxuries this place offers. We don't have to think about police work or crime until Carter picks us up in the morning. So, how about enjoying the whirlpool, then choosing a movie to watch? Maybe a comedy? I saw several of those on the shelf."

"Isn't it too soon after a meal to go in the water? My mother always used to say we couldn't go swimming until an hour after a meal."

"Carrie, it's just a big bath tub! Besides, I don't think people believe that warning about swimming any more. So, will you join me?"

She looked up at him, winked, and began unbuttoning her blouse. "Well, only if you promise to save me from drowning."

DANIELLE REPRISE

Since both she and Henry were early risers, Carrie had a lot of time the next morning to prepare herself for being a calm, cool, experienced professional around Detective Art Carter. She would not let who he was spoil her demeanor. He couldn't change who *she* was.

Her good intentions almost crashed when his knock came at 9:30–loud, aggressive, repeated. It sounded so typical of the man. *Okay, you don't have to like him to be professional.*

"Henry, are you ready?"

"In a minute."

Another knock, louder. Obviously opening the door was up to her. *Okay. Calm, cool, collected. Who cares how he knocks?*

She jumped back when she opened the door and Captain Doug Boinevich's next knock barely missed her face.

"Oh, whoa. Sorry Ms., er, Carrie. I didn't know how well sound would travel through these solid doors, so I...."

Her laughter stopped him. That's when she discovered tough-looking Captain Doug Boinevich had a lovely rosy blush.

Behind her, Henry said, "I think I missed something. Doug, are you flirting with my wife?"

"Absolutely not, Major King. I wouldn't dare, as tempting as it might be. Ready to go?"

"We are," Henry said. "Glad to see you, but where's

Carter? Seems to me you're getting more on-the-street time than would be usual."

"An interview opportunity came up for a case he's working on, and he said it was urgent. The person he needs to talk with is in a hospital down in Joplin. Her injuries were serious, and she's been unconscious for a week. They called him early this morning to say she's awake, so he got on the road south before daylight. There really wasn't time to change plans after I heard about it, and, since I'm up on the details of the Hawkins case, I decided to come along as your chaperone instead."

He laughed, but Carrie wondered if he really thought of himself as being there to keep both of them on the straight and narrow when it came to a conversation with Danielle Hawkins.

Possibly because of new-found comfort in his role as a valuable supplement to police department capabilities, Henry ignored the chaperone comment and kept to the high ground. "Fine. We can talk about procedures on the way."

Once they were seated in the car, with Carrie in back and the two men in front, Boinevich said, "How about Carrie as lead? I never met Ms. Hawkins, and she might be more comfortable with a female anyway. That okay?"

"Okay," she said, wondering how she could talk to Danielle with Boinevich present and be sure the woman didn't reveal they had spoken before. Carrie wished she'd thought to tell Henry she'd like to manage a few minutes alone with Danielle before the four of them got together.

Boinevich continued, "We want to find out what she

knows about any of the open cases involving her family–
possible burglary, plus selling stolen goods and a
murder. Quite a few items from the stash in Gordon's car
and home have already been identified as stolen. You
know where they came from? Mostly small-town
historical museums in Missouri and Kansas. None of the
museums had many items of significant value and, in
every case, their security was minimum or non-existent.
Easy pickings. The thief or thieves simply took the best
and left the rest. It's suspected some of the items were
actually removed in broad daylight when the museums
were open. Nothing definite on any of those cases yet,
but a couple of the museum attendants remembered a
pregnant woman and her husband were among visitors
the day their things were stolen. All of the reported
burglaries took place over the past two years.

"There was also some jewelry and other items that
came from home burglaries here in Kansas City, but the
owners reported a lot more items than Gordon had at the
house. Probably Graham already sold quite a bit of that
stuff.

"One big puzzle is who's head of this operation, and
head over what? Is there a connection with several
burglars, and Graham was just fencing their take, or was
he a burglar himself? In any case, Cousin Graham seems
the obvious pick as boss. But, if he's the big cheese, why
was he killed? Someone else wants to take over? Is
Gordon next in line for boss? He seems more like a naive
dupe than anything, but maybe that's just an act. Was he
knowingly selling stolen goods?

"And, what about Danielle? From what I've heard, she's sharper than her husband, and she is the one who kept records of purchases and sales for their shop, including what they bought from Graham. After the murder did she convince good old Gordon that they could now sell Graham's remaining merchandise? Did she know, or at least suspect, that it was stolen? And, I wonder if she knows anything about a storage location for Graham's merchandise. Does she have a key or keys to it from that nail in Graham's closet, or was the nail merely a left-over from previous owners of the house and never used by any Hawkins?"

"That's at least a dozen questions," Carrie said, "Quite a few things."

"Hope for the moon and be glad when you get a pinch of star dust." Boinevich said.

She nodded, thinking the captain not only blushed prettily, he could speak in poetry. "Is it okay if I tell Danielle you now know the merchandise in her home and Gordon's car was stolen, and where some of it came from?"

Boinevich considered this for a moment, then said, "I think yes. Might help in getting answers."

"Okay, then I suggest, if you trust me, that you and Henry act like you're not paying much attention to us at first. Maybe you could let us hear you sharing a bit of guy-talk that has nothing to do with the case. We can probably sit at adjoining tables in the snack area. Let what's going on lead us—do you know what I mean? If she tightens up and doesn't say much from the beginning, that's when you chat guy-stuff while she and I get acquainted, so to speak. Later, if she opens up, I can ask one of you a question, or something, and you'd then begin to take part in whatever's going on."

"See, I told you she's a natural," Henry said, smiling at her across the seat back.

Boinevich laughed. "Yes, my friend, and here we are at the museum. Let's have a go at Ms. Hawkins."

Carrie jumped out of the car ahead of the men, hoping Henry would catch on that she needed time alone with Danielle. On the way in, he stopped to point out something across the square to Boinevich, and she hurried in, rushing past the ticket clerk who simply gaped at her. Boinevich could explain when he came in. She sighed with relief when she saw Danielle arranging merchandise in a gift shop display, while the dark-haired and well-endowed clerk named Kinley helped the only customer at the counter, a good-looking male.

Though Danielle looked up quickly, she didn't have time to show any emotion at all before Carrie said in a rush, "I've heard what happened with Gordon yesterday. Believe me, the police don't know I've talked with you, and now they want me to ask you a few questions about their case. Please don't give away we've talked...." She saw Henry and Doug entering the shop, and finished, "...talk a bit, if you don't mind. Can you take a break?"

Danielle turned toward Kinley and started to speak, but the young woman had already glanced away from her customer to give Carrie a quick, appraising look. She then nodded a quick affirmation to Danielle and returned to her animated conversation with the man.

As soon as they were in the seating area, Carrie introduced Henry and his friend, Captain Doug Boinevich. After Danielle said she didn't want anything to eat or drink, the men went to get coffee and donuts for themselves.

Still speaking quickly, Carrie said, "The police have discovered that the items from Graham's room and Gordon's car were stolen. Many of them came from small museums in Missouri and Kansas, or from home burglaries in the Kansas City area."

Danielle bit her lip, "Well, from what I saw of the things in those boxes, I guess that makes sense. But where did he get the stuff he sold me? It sure wasn't from any museum."

"Maybe some of his merchandise really was stock from distressed merchants."

"All I bought from him looked like that, but...what was in his room... well, I dunno."

"Which means he must have had another storage place. Do you still have the key that you found in his closet?"

"Yeah. It's in my purse. I haven't had any luck finding what it fits. There are so many storage places around the area, and they wouldn't let me inside the fence at most of the ones I've tried."

"Now that the cat is out of the bag about stolen goods, you should turn the key over to the police. They can probably find out what it unlocks pretty quickly."

"Yeah, I guess so."

Carrie checked to be sure the men were still involved in donut selection before she went on."What about the jewelry you mentioned yesterday? Are you sure it was costume?"

"Some of it was, or Graham wouldn't have sold it to me cheap enough to put in our shop. But there's good stuff too. She held out her arm. "Here, this bangle bracelet was one of his pieces."

Carrie studied it. "Gosh, Danielle, that's beautiful. It's real gold, isn't it? And it looks old."

Danielle turned the bracelet on her wrist. "Don't know what it's worth, but I like it."

"Me, too. Now, are you sure you don't remember anything more about Graham's business or what happened in Van Buren?"

"I've thought and thought since we talked..." She looked up as the two men took seats at a table next to them. "All else I can remember is that once, when I was cleaning up our storage area in the shop, I found some little printed cardboard tags with dates on them that I knew weren't from our stock. Now that you mention museums I can figure what they were, because we have a few tags kinda like that around this museum. You know, telling what something is, stuff like that."

Carrie and Danielle both glanced over at the men before Carrie asked, "Do you still have those?"

"They're at the house. I kept them because they were so odd. I thought about asking Graham if he knew what they were from, but something about him always scared me. I figured the less said the better."

"Did you show them to Gordon?"

"Nope. That would have been the same as showing them to Graham."

Danielle's hands were folded on the table, and Carrie reached out, covering them with her own hands.

"While you were thinking things over, did you recall anything at all that might give us a clue to why Graham was killed? The tiniest thing might help."

Danielle was silent, looking down at their hands. When she looked up, she turned toward the next table and said, "You guys might as well join us, I don't have anything to hide."

Carrie moved around to sit next to Danielle, then Henry and Doug took the two remaining chairs at their table. Henry said, "Thanks, Ms. Hawkins."

"It's Danielle. Well, when Graham was packing to go to Van Buren that last time, I went to his room with a shirt he'd asked me to iron, and I saw him putting a little gun in his bag. I musta gasped, or something, because he knew I saw what he had. He kinda laughed, and said 'Dani, I always carry insurance.' I just handed him the shirt and left the room, and that was it."

Doug Boinevich asked, "Do you remember what the gun looked like?"

"I don't know much about guns, but it looked fancy to me. Wasn't too big. Had twisty lines and some leaves cut into the silver metal on the sides. The handle was dirty plastic."

"Ah," Henry said, and they all looked at him, but he simply shook his head.

After a minute, Carrie said, "Danielle told me about a bit of evidence at her home that may be helpful to you in the burglary case. They're probably labels from a museum display, and she found them in their shop's storage area. She didn't realize what they were until I told her about some of Graham's goods being stolen from museums. Do you want her to bring them to work tomorrow so an officer can pick them up?"

"I'm off tomorrow, they can come to my house in the morning."

The captain nodded, and Carrie went on, "If Captain Boinevich or other police officers want you to explain to them again what you've told me today, that's okay, isn't it?"

"Yeah, I guess it's okay."

Led by Carrie, they all stood. She wrapped Danielle in a hug, and said, "Thank you so much, you've been a big help. And now, I think it would be best if you gave Captain Boinevich the key from Graham's closet."

"If you'll come back to the gift shop with me, I'll get it."

THE KEY TO...

"I don't see it," Danielle said as she peered into her purse and pushed the contents around. "I've been keeping it with my coins, but it musta slipped out and gotten mixed up with all the other stuff in here."

She looked up as Kinley tapped her on the arm. "Danielle, we've got people waiting, can you...?"

"Oh gosh, I'm sorry, I'll be right there."

Danielle bent to return her purse to its place under the counter and said, "I can't dump it all out here. Would you guys like to tour the museum until I can get away and look through everything?" She was saying "May I help you?" to a nearby couple before Carrie, Henry, and Doug left the counter.

"We might as well show you the scene of the crime," Henry said, as they walked out of the gift shop.

When the three of them were standing next to the railing by the boat ride pool, Captain Boinevich looked at Carrie and said, "Well, the railing is too high for anyone to simply push you over. Whoever it was had to lift you, and do it quickly. Those display cases over there would have hidden part of what was going on from a couple of directions but straight back there's a clear view. Because of the circumstances, Ms. Hawkins is the most likely candidate for doing the dumping. No one else involved, other than maybe Gordon, knew you were here, and he was in Van Buren. How long had you been in the museum when you got dumped?"

"Oh, probably an hour and a half or two hours. Does

231

that sound right, Henry?"

"Yes, and it couldn't have been more than fifteen minutes after Danielle cornered Carrie in the restroom."

"Okay, two hours would be enough time for someone to get to the museum after you arrived, assuming they were in the city to begin with, and of course we don't know how many people are involved yet. But, if someone did come here, seems Danielle would have been the one to alert him...or her."

Carrie shook her head. "I'm just sure it couldn't have been Danielle."

"Don't be too sure," the captain said as they moved away from the railing. "Let's take a few minutes for a quick look around the museum, then go back up and see if Danielle's found that key. I'm betting she hasn't. Gordon could have easily removed it from her purse, or she might have left it at home and has no intention of giving it to us."

Carrie wished she could tell the captain that Danielle had mentioned having the key in her purse yesterday, but to do so would reveal they'd talked. And that would expose, not only her, but Henry, as being willing to hide evidence from the police. She didn't think even the friendly captain would like that.

"I don't think she's told her husband about finding it yet," was all she said.

"Likely there are two keys anyway," Henry added. "The other might have been in Graham's pocket when he was killed, but everything other than the buttons had been removed before we found him."

"Those buttons are sure a peculiarity," was Doug Boinevich's only comment.

* * *

As soon as they returned to the gift shop, Danielle greeted them with a lift of her shoulders and a helpless, palms-out gesture. "I can't find it," she said. "I'll look at home tonight. Maybe I can give it to the officer who picks up those museum tags in the morning."

"Does Gordon know you have the key?" Carrie asked.

"He didn't, but when the guys found that nail inside Graham's closet yesterday, he guessed about it and asked me if I had seen a key there."

"And?"

"Well, I had to tell him, didn't I? I was kinda surprised when he didn't seem too interested after that, but he was pretty wrung out after all that happened yesterday. Just ate his supper, then sat staring at the television set and drinking beer until we went to bed."

"Could he have gotten in your purse without you knowing?"

"Sure. I don't hide it. But I don't think he'd have any better luck learning what that key fits than I did. I hope the police can figure out what it's to. And I hope someone will tell me about it when they do."

With that, she turned away to help another customer.

As they left the museum, Henry said, "Doug, I don't see what more Carrie and I can add to your research here. I know there's no real resolution yet, but unless you think of some way we can be of further service to you, we may as well head back home in the morning. So, will you take us to the station to pick up our car?"

The captain answered without a thought, "Okay. I agree with your assessment, but both Deputy Chief Duncan and I are puzzled about the Van Buren connection. That's out of our jurisdiction, but it isn't out of yours. Maybe, working with Sgt. Burke, you can find some answers there that will help us here."

"Very possibly. Let's see... learn more about dealers there who may have bought from Graham or Gordon, see if any dealers admit to knowing either man, buying from them, or just talking with them. Plus, who saw Graham on the day he died? That kind of thing?"

"Sounds good."

As Doug pulled up next to their car, Henry said, "We'll be in touch as soon as we learn anything new, and will you let us know what more you uncover here?"

"Right. See you the next time you're this way, and thanks to both of you for all your help."

As soon as they were in their suite, Carrie said, "We really could check out now and head for home. It's less than a five-hour drive."

"I know, but what do you think about getting in touch with the Duncans and see if we can take them out to dinner this evening?

"Great idea. Do you know a place?"

"There was a barbecue joint the three of us used to favor with our presence fairly frequently, and I'd like to introduce it to you. I'll check the phone book to see if it's still open. Then, after we get back here, you and I can enjoy one more time in the whirlpool tub."

"Maybe we should have one of those put in at home."

"Hmmm."

As he picked up the phone book, Carrie thought about barbecue, a food form that was relatively new in her life. Eleanor and Shirley had introduced it to her at Bubba's, a barbecue restaurant in Eureka Springs, when the three of them were there planning her wedding to Henry at the Crescent Hotel. Her parents never ate barbecue, and Amos McCrite looked down on it as food for the underclasses. She wasn't yet totally enthusiastic about this medium for presenting meat on a plate, but did love the beans that always came along as a side dish.

She had changed to thinking about where they might put a whirlpool tub in their bathroom without giving up closet space when Henry said, "All fixed. We're to pick up the Duncans at their house at 5:45, and I made reservations for 6:30 at the restaurant, allowing time for driving in traffic."

"Good. Huggy Bear, would you do us a favor? I'm hungry now, and I bet you are too, since we missed lunch. I want to check our phone calls at home as well as e-mail, so would you mind going to the dining room while I do that, and see what snacks they've set out for guests today? I'm not particular, but fruit yogurt and carrot sticks would be nice if they have them, and some of the wheat crackers. Okay?"

"You bet. Maybe they'll have those pastrami sandwich bites and fudge cake again."

Ohh, the fudge cake. "Fudge cake for me, too, if you please, or cookies would be okay. The tray is over there."

* * *

When she opened the door to his knock several minutes later Henry immediately noticed her perplexed look. "What's up?"

"Funniest thing. Jenni Lively had called me at home. She said she's sure I realize a lot of her stock comes from estate sales, and now relatives of someone who's estate was auctioned a few months ago want her to return the pendant I bought in her shop. Evidently they allowed it to go in their sale by mistake. She's asked me to bring it to her within a few days, and promised to buy it back for $150 to cover my trouble."

He put the tray down on their sitting room table and tapped two fingers across his mouth while he thought. Then he said, "Let's look at that necklace again. I admit I never studied it up close. Have you?"

"Well yes, sort of. It's well made, if that's what you mean."

"$50.00 well-made or possibly better?"

"Golly, I don't know. I did think it was a good buy."

He sat at the table, picked up a finger sandwich, and ate it without paying much attention to the taste. A feeling of unease was building in his thoughts, and it was strong enough to overcome recognition of excellent pastrami.

Carrie sat down and laid the pendant on the table between them. They both studied it in silence while she opened her cup of yogurt. Finally he picked the pendant up, turned it over, and said, "I wish I had a magnifying glass."

"You think it's a real... whatever... emerald?"

His unease increased. "Maybe. I'm sure no expert. The gold work looks very well done–maybe too nice for a synthetic stone? I wonder if it really came from an estate sale."

"Golly. Do you think we should take it to a jeweler and find out what it is? I never thought about it being a real gem of any kind, and now I sure hope it isn't."

"A jeweler could evaluate it, but if it is real, I don't want us to be the ones who find that out." He thought for a moment, then said, "Ray said Rose admired your necklace, so tonight, I suggest you give it to her."

"*Henry!*"

He'd anticipated her protest. "Cara, if it's real, it's possibly stolen, which means you have no right to it. It could be part of this case, and it may even be what the person who caused the fire alarm was searching for. We'll explain the circumstances to the Duncans. If it isn't real, I am sure Rose will return it to you... or she can keep it and we'll find you another."

"I love the color...."

"I know, I know, and it sure does match your eyes. I'm sorry. But after tonight you can honestly tell Ms. Lively that you gave the necklace to a friend. No need to mention names. I suspect we'll both be much better off if we don't have that necklace in our possession. And Ray can handle the evaluation and research as to whether or not it's stolen. It'll be out of our hands."

"Oh," she said in a very little voice that made him wish he had enough money to buy a blue-green emerald for her.

A JEWEL TO DIE FOR

Deputy Chief Rayford Duncan wiped his fingers on the wet towel a server had just provided and said, "Mmm mmm good. Rose and I kinda forgot about this place after you left, Hank. It's great to be back, and their brisket is every bit as tasty as I remember."

"It is good," Carrie agreed. "As a newcomer to barbecue, I can't be a real judge, but I'd sure order what I just ate again. In fact, I might even come back to Kansas City to eat here... and see you folks, of course."

"You'd better say that, girlfriend." Rose smiled at Carrie, took a sip of iced tea, and continued, "We want to see you two here at least twice a year, which doesn't seem too unreasonable now that you've turned up a daughter and grandson to visit. Lots of reasons to come back, and it isn't all that far."

Henry, who was dabbing at a big splotch of barbecue sauce on his shirt, said, "I should know better than to order ribs. I do it every time, and I make a mess every time. It wasn't so bad when my uniform shirts went to the cleaners and Irena's maids did my civilian clothes, but now Carrie and I are the household laundry service. How do you get this stuff out?"

Carrie studied the rust-colored blob, and winked at Rose. "I suggest we cut the spot out, then I can applique a contrasting patch there. Start a new style. Patchwork chic."

Rose laughed. "Well now, that is a creative idea for sure."

"Okay, down to serious business," Henry said, setting aside his napkin after one last dab at the stain. "You know the story of the pendant and why Rose now has it in her purse. Any new thoughts, Ray?"

"We'll have it appraised, and check to see if it's been reported stolen. If we find it on our list, then we'll get in touch with Burke and ask him to question Ms. Lively, look over her stock pretty carefully, and perhaps charge her with possession of stolen goods." He turned to Carrie. "You were looking at stolen jewelry on the Internet? What did you learn?"

"Here's my report on the afternoon's search, sir," she said as she took a small notebook from her purse. "I started out by typing in 'stolen jewelry.' 466,000 places to check there, so I narrowed it down by trying 'jewelry stolen in the Kansas City area.' That got me down to 8,880. Trying again, I asked about 'emerald jewelry stolen in the Kansas City area.' That reduced it to an almost workable 3,100 sites, so I started looking down that list. I saw a lot of breathtakingly beautiful jewelry, but nothing like my pendant. I got through about 500 of the posts before my eyes and head decided they couldn't take any more. A lot of the listings turned out to be jewelry store ads, and, fairly frequently, I was warned that a certain site was unsafe for various reasons. My word Ray, how does your burglary division ever keep up with it all? And why jewelry store listings among information about stolen jewelry? It's bewildering. The store ads seemed to me to be either blatant offers to sell stolen goods, or an invitation to thieves."

"Well now, if you're looking to buy costly jewelry at a discount price and don't see what you want in the–shall we say–underground market, you just might think about looking in real jewelry stores. Too bad that all sorts of stolen items, including archeological treasures looted from sites around the world, are now offered for sale on the Internet. If you're already searching there for jewelry, what better place for a store to post an ad? But you're right, it could be an invitation to thieves."

"I sure saw pictures of some fabulous stuff, beautiful almost beyond what this simple female could grasp." She looked at Rose. "I saw a pair of cuff bracelets so loaded with emeralds, rubies, sapphires, and diamonds that there was no metal showing. And they were each over an inch wide! Stolen two years ago, never found."

"I'd be scared to go out of the house wearing something like that," Rose said, "and I'd feel embarrassed and almost sinful over all that show."

"Me, too. So, Ray, do you want me to keep looking?"

"Wait until our guys have a chance to check your pendant."

"Rose's pendant now."

Ray slid over in the booth and put an arm around his wife. "Carrie, I have a strong feeling neither your nor Rose will ever get to wear that necklace. You two had better shop for something more in the price range your poor husbands can afford."

Henry said, "I hate to bring this evening to a close, but Carrie and I plan to be on the road fairly early in the morning. Ray, will you keep in touch about the pendant?

We took a picture of it before we brought it to you tonight, in case that might be of use to us, but would you e-mail me an official photo when you have one? Carrie and I will probably make a trip to Van Buren to consult with Sgt. Burke in the near future. I'd like to know more about the necklace before we go there, and also know what's pending between the sergeant and Ms. Lively."

"You've got it. Hey buddy, thanks for the wonderful evening. I echo Rose's request that you come back for a visit soon. Until I retire, it'll be easier for you to travel than for us."

"We do expect you at Blackberry Hollow whenever you can make it," Carrie said, "though it's nothing like Kansas City."

"And that's not all bad," Ray said. "We look forward to a visit."

* * *

"I'll be glad to get home," Carrie said as they crossed the border from Missouri into Arkansas, "but I sure did like staying at that bed and breakfast. I wonder what they charge for regular guests?"

"I asked," Henry told her. "Rounds off to $350 a night and up, plus extras, of course."

"Ouch."

"Uh-huh."

"Wonder if we could manage to need police protection on our next trip to Kansas City?"

"Don't even think it. You want a potty stop yet?"

"Nope, I'm good 'til we get home."

Henry pulled into their garage an hour later and,

after they finished unloading the car, he said, "I'm going to fix a Pepsi; you want something to drink?"

"Thanks, I'll join you as soon as I hang these things in the closet."

He was back almost immediately. "Cara, could you come to the kitchen for a minute?"

"Coming. What's up?"

When she joined him, he pointed to a few tiny brown flecks in the sink. "That's coffee. Could you have spilled it there before we went to Kansas City?"

"No, I wasn't in the can of coffee then. Remember, we used one-cup coffee bags that morning."

"Oh, yeah, we did. Then how about this?" He pointed to the counter.

"How about what?"

"Here... a bit of spilled sugar. Hard to see, but you can feel it."

"Henry, I don't put sugar in my coffee, as you know. Why do you ask?"

"I just wanted to be sure before... well, I wonder if someone was in the house while we were gone. Were Shirley or Eleanor coming in to check on things?"

"No. Could it have been a mouse or something? FatCat wasn't here."

"Not that kind of mess. I think we'd better give the house a good search, including a look in all the drawers and storage boxes. You'd best check your own stuff. I can't be sure how normal would look. See if everything is just like you left it."

"Well okay, but why survey the whole house over a

bit of spilled sugar and coffee?"

"Because, my love, thieves as well as law-enforcement people know that homeowners often hide jewelry and other small, expensive items in ice cube trays, cans of coffee, and kitchen canisters. Unexplained spilled sugar and a few scattered coffee grounds say to me someone with that knowledge searched through our kitchen, and it's easy to assume they were looking for the pendant. When that person or persons didn't find it in the kitchen, they would have gone through the rest of the house. They didn't intend for us to know they'd been here, that's why we didn't catch on right away."

"How could they get in the house? The windows and doors are okay. Everything was closed and locked when we got home."

"I know. But my key ring was on the desk by our computer when we left the room during that fake fire alarm. Someone in the know could have made an impression of our house key and had it duplicated. Very easy in and out. Leaving the keys there didn't worry me earlier because I couldn't see why anyone would notice or care. But now...."

"I'll call a locksmith right away."

"Person who did this won't be back, but that's a good idea anyway."

She knew she sounded calm—simply taking a wise step in the face of what had happened. The weeping and wailing were all inside her head. Someone had been inside her home and probably went through most of her possessions. Where had this person searched, what did he touch?

She wondered if Henry would understand when she threw out the contents of all her canisters.

Calmly she asked, "How about fingerprints?"

"I'd bet there aren't any. This thief was most certainly too smart for that. Okay, let's search the house."

Thirty minutes later Carrie reported the only things she noticed awry were tangled necklace chains in her jewelry chest and a scattered stack of once neatly folded panties in her underwear drawer. "But both of those could be my fault. I was in the chest and my underwear drawer when I packed for the trip. As you know, all my good jewelry is in my safe deposit box. I'm glad about that now."

Henry said, "I don't think the object of this search was general burglary, and I couldn't find anything disturbed at all in my stuff. Carrie, someone sure wants that necklace back."

"Should we phone the sheriff's office?"

"I don't think they'd take kindly to being called out for nothing more than a kitchen spill. But I am going to call Ray." He went to the phone.

* * *

As soon as Ray Duncan heard Henry's voice he said, "I was just getting ready to call you. What's up?"

Henry explained about the search.

"Huh. This gets stickier and stickier, and your gut feeling about that pendant was right. It's a good quality emerald, possible value at least $25,000. Came from a jewelry store in the Plaza, not a house burglary. Stolen two years ago. Most of the stuff was recovered after an anonymous tip saying where the thieves had stashed it, but the necklace and a couple more high dollar items were never found. Insurance company paid off."

"Who worked the case?"

"Carter and his partner then, Louie Drum. Why?"

"I guess Drum's another one I don't remember."

"He was in the reserves. Called up shortly after that. Died in Afghanistan."

"Sorry to hear it. Did you catch the thieves?"

"No, not for that particular case. It dried up shortly after Carter and Drum found the stash. A lot of fairly recent jewelry thefts around here have seemed similar enough that I would have thought we were dealing with a single gang. In each of those cases we've ended up recovering a good portion of the stolen items but never all of them. Frustrating."

"And you've caught no one?"

"I didn't say that. Carter did get a few two-bit guys, most working singly. All of them insisted they were operating independently, and none of them admitted to being responsible for more than two of the burglaries. Some even had alibis to prove it. Each must have had inside knowledge of the places they hit, and Carter never figured out where they got that."

"Could there be a boss over all of them? Like, say, Graham Hawkins?"

"Yeah, maybe he's a possible. I think there's gotta be someone over all this. It seems too slick for the guys we've caught. Carter disagrees with me—and with Doug

Boinevich, by the way. Doug sees a mastermind over the thefts, same as I do.

"Does this apply to the museum thefts, too?"

"I don't know. Whoever pulled those off had to be pretty darn cool since they operated in broad daylight. Lots of research there, just like the home and jewelry store burglaries here in Kansas City."

"Have there been any recent burglaries of this type reported?"

"No, though there were a couple right after Graham's murder."

"Ah. A lot to think about." After a moment's silence, Henry said, "Have you called Sgt. Burke about Lively and the necklace yet?"

"Left that to Carter."

"Carrie and I will go down there, probably tomorrow. I just wanted to be sure Burke knew the latest before we talked to him about coming. I don't want to get in the way of the Van Buren PD. So, could you let me know for sure when Carter has contacted him? Then we can follow up."

"I'll get back to you about that ASAP, and I'm sending you a picture of the pendant."

"Thanks. Anything else I should know?"

"Yes. Danielle never found that key and we questioned Gordon pretty closely. Put a bit of pressure on him. He denies having ever seen it. We got the museum tags from her, though, and I assume they'll tie to one of the museum burglaries we spoke about."

"Hm. Maybe there's still a duplicate key somewhere

in Van Buren."

"Possible. Okay, buddy. Be careful down there. Wouldn't hurt to carry some protection for a while. Is your retired officer's carry permit up-to-date?"

"Yes, but...."

"Doesn't mean you'll have to use a gun. I just want you and Carrie to be safe, okay?"

Henry didn't answer.

After an awkward pause, Ray Duncan closed the conversation. "Well then, I'll sign off for now. Boinevich or I will get back to you later this afternoon about Carter's contact with Burke."

Henry repeated the new information to Carrie, leaving out Ray's question about his carry permit. Following her brief "whew" over the value of the pendant, they sat in silence on their couch. Finally she said, "Uh, about Detective Carter... am I the only one with a funny feeling? Y'know, during that fire scare I saw a fireman who had a strut like Carter. Couldn't have told who it was though, because of the helmet, face gear, and all. He did have on athletic shoes rather than boots."

"You never mentioned that."

"I didn't really think about it until now."

"I see. Yes, I see." He frowned, leaned back on the couch, and shut his eyes.

SUSPICIOUS MINDS

Carrie, her own forehead wrinkled in perturbed contemplation, watched her husband frown for a few minutes before she decided thinking about Detective Art Carter wasn't proving all that productive.

When she could stand the silence no longer, she said, "I think I'll call Ms. Lively and tell her I gave the pretty cut glass pendant to a friend. I might even tell her the friend's husband is a police chief. Or should I wait until we visit her tomorrow? What do you think?"

Henry opened his eyes and sat up straighter on the couch, still frowning. Finally he said, "I'd like to see her reaction when you tell her the pendant is out of reach. I'm sure she's unhappy, possibly even in trouble, because she sold it for a tiny fraction of its true worth."

"Henry, I feel sorry for her. I don't know how she got the emerald, but obviously she had no more idea than I about the value."

"I'm sure she didn't, and she won't know yet that we are aware it's not costume jewelry. But tracing the necklace back to its source would certainly give the guys in Kansas City valuable information, and I'm hoping we can do that through her. Maybe saying you gave it away will startle her enough that, before she has time to think things through, she'll drop her estate sale story and tell us where the emerald really came from, or at least identify who sold it to her. She may want to impress on us the importance of returning it. I'm sure whoever supplied her with the piece is saying she needs to get it back from you."

Carrie stared at Henry, searching for hope behind his words and not finding it. "She's not in danger is she?"

"I wouldn't think so, but someone else has gotten involved quite recently since she didn't know the value of the pendant when she sold it to you. I think our mastermind learned she'd sold it and what the selling price was. He must have told her to get it back, even though it could have been his mistake—or Graham Hawkins's—that she had it in the first place. I'm guessing it was mixed in with a lot of costume jewelry, perhaps as a clever way to hide it."

"You're talking recent time. Does that mean you've ruled out Cousin Graham?"

"A living mastermind is still very much in evidence."

"Gordon doesn't fit the mastermind image, does he?"

"No. Danielle is smart enough and ambitious enough to fit the part, but from what you've said, I'm leaving her out of consideration, at least for now."

"Carter?"

"I just don't know, Carrie. I hate thinking about that, but there are... peculiarities."

She changed the subject." We still don't know whether or not Jenni Lively is providing a willing outlet for stolen merchandise."

"True, but remember, somehow she knew or learned that Gordon's cousin was the dead man on the riverbank. How? And why didn't she tell the police rather than calling Gordon?

"I'd like to find out how Carter and Burke plan to

proceed before we get too nosy with her or anyone else. We'll see what Ray can tell us when he calls. But, no matter what, I see nothing wrong in going to Van Buren in response to Lively's call asking for the return of the pendant. That's our personal business.

"Are either the Booths or Stacks available tomorrow? I think appearing in a group might be more daunting to Ms. Lively than just the two of us walking in her store. She can't keep her eyes on everyone while you or I talk with her and the rest fan out to look over her stock. If she knows what's been going on, she might think we're searching for stolen items."

"Not to mention there's safety in numbers?"

"That, too. But I don't anticipate trouble or I wouldn't invite others to go along. After all, we haven't the power to arrest anyone."

"Does Mastermind know that?"

"Of course."

"Will Mastermind consider us a threat?"

And that was the problem jabbing at Henry, though he said nothing.

She looked at him, brow furrowed, then said. "When I phoned to tell Eleanor we were home, she was almost too busy to talk. She said they were preparing for a big wedding and reception on Saturday. Jason is helping her start the set-up tomorrow. I don't know about the Booths, but we need to drive down there anyway, give them our gifts, and pick up FatCat."

"Good. I'm looking forward to seeing Roger's reaction to the steamboat book."

As soon as they started down the hill toward Walden Creek and the Booth's farm, Carrie said, "Look! Color is beginning to show on top of the bluffs. Some yellow, and there's orange and red in the tupelo-gum."

Henry didn't answer. He was still thinking about Mastermind.

Roger came out of the dairy barn and waved while Carrie was shooing a couple of cows away from the Booth's front gate. He walked toward the house as Henry pulled the car through and Carrie fastened the gate. As soon as they were parked and out of the car, Roger said, "Sorry about the reception committee. Lulu has just been bred for the first time, and Mary Belle is here to keep her company. Dang bull chased Lulu all over the barnyard and she didn't take kindly to his attentions."

"Did he—?" Henry began.

"Oh, yeah. Got her cornered, but right now she's mad at all of us. I brought Mary Belle in to help calm her down. We'll see how things went in a few weeks."

He sat in a chair on the wide porch and pulled off his boots, replacing them with worn leather house slippers. "Y'all come on in. Smells like Shirley's baking cookies."

In a couple of minutes the four of them were seated at the Booth's kitchen table enjoying the spicy-sweet fragrance of oatmeal cookies Shirley deemed "too hot to eat yet." While they were waiting, Carrie opened her tote bag, handed a box with the button pin in it to Shirley, put two steamboat mugs on the scrubbed oak table, and gave Henry's purchase, *Steamboats on the Western Rivers* by Louis C. Hunter, to Roger.

"Well now, this is great," Roger said. "These here steamboats on the cover have smokestacks that look about the size of the pipe we saw in the middle of that island. But, why 'western rivers?'"

"Seems odd to us now," Henry said, "but Hunter is referring to the west as people living in the east defined it in the mid-19th century. It wasn't just Montana and Wyoming, buffalo and American Indians. The Mississippi Valley was 'west' to many people. Look in the index under 'Arkansas.'"

Roger obeyed, and whistled. "I see what you mean. There's a lot here about the Arkansas River. Reckon we'll find something about the *Sarah Anne?*"

"I didn't see the name, but I haven't read it all. I got a copy of the book for myself, too."

Shirley held the button pin toward Roger, "Look here. Now I can wear this and, when folks ask about it, I'll be able to tell them the story of Great-grampy's adventures during the war." She looked over at Carrie and Henry. "These gifts are mighty fine, and we're grateful for them. Now, anyone ready for cookies?"

While they were eating, Carrie and Henry shared highlights of their recent experiences, ending with Ray Duncan's information about the value of the pendant.

"Whoo-eee," Shirley said, "you sure did have some adventures. And, why on earth would anyone want something worth that much? Waste of good money."

"Well, it is a beautiful thing," Carrie said, "but I admit I liked it better when I thought it was just a nice piece of costume jewelry. Now I want nothing to do with it."

"Except to find out who stole it and how it got to Van Buren," Henry said.

Roger said, "Reckon we need to go talk with that Ms. Lively, don't we?"

Henry laughed."I thought *we* might. Can you get away tomorrow?"

"Junior and the hired man both took off today. They can get along without us tomorrow."

"Pick you up about 7:30? And we thank you for keeping FatCat. Where is she?"

"Last I saw she was in her usual place on the back of our sofa."

Though she protested over being removed from her perch, FatCat was purring in Henry's lap by the time they drove through the farm gate. "Good thing I don't have to shift," he said.

An hour later, Deputy Chief Duncan called to tell Henry that Detective Carter asked him to inform "Mr. and Mrs. King" their help was no longer required, and he would do any follow-up necessary through official channels in Van Buren.

"Has he talked to Burke yet?"

"I don't know."

"Do you think he's planning a trip to Van Buren?"

"I don't know that either, but I'd say it's likely."

Henry's thoughts were racing now. So Carter didn't want them back in Van Buren. He said, "Can you find something vital for him to do in Kansas City tomorrow?"

"What's this about, Hank?"

"Not sure yet. But I have another favor. E-mail us a photo of Carter."

"Are you thinking what I think you're thinking?"

Henry hadn't formed an answer when Ray said, "How sure are you?"

"I'm not sure at all. It is just thinking right now. But if you consider the details of this case, beginning with police visits to the Hawkins's shop and the warnings Graham got over the phone, well... see what you come up with. Then there's the skillful search of our house, and his trip to Joplin, not that far from Blackberry Hollow. He could have rented a car in Joplin to keep extra mileage off his police vehicle. And, here's information you don't have. Carrie told me today she thought she saw Carter dressed in fire department gear the night of the smoke bomb event."

"Ah."

"We've already planned a trip to Van Buren with friends tomorrow. Carrie will tell Jenni Lively she gave the green glass pendant to a friend, so can't return it. We're especially interested in the kind of reaction we get to that news. Then we'll shop for something to replace the pendant. Lively carries a lot of costume jewelry. Carrie says she didn't think she saw anything of high-dollar value when she was in the shop last summer, though of course there was the pendant. We'll look more carefully this time. Who knows?"

"Let's pretend I didn't hear you say what your plans are. Whatever you do tomorrow, be careful. In the meantime I can do a little checking at this end.

"I'll get that photo of Carter to you in a few minutes. I've got one in my computer from a party last Christmas, so I don't have to use police files."

"Thanks, Ray. After our trip tomorrow I hope we'll have some concrete information to give you. By the way, do you have a record of where Art Carter was on July 17th and 18th?"

"That's when Graham Hawkins was killed?"

"Right."

"Whee-you...this is sticky."

"I know."

"Well, okay, but good buddy, you watch your backside."

"Just be sure Carter stays there tomorrow."

"For sure, and I'll check about July 17th and 18th. I'll send an answer with the photo."

"Appreciate it."

"Hank?"

"What?"

"Oh, nuts. Just call me as soon as you can tomorrow."

WHERE IS THE KILLER?

When Ray's e-mail arrived, Carrie stared at the Christmas party photo in stunned silence for a full minute before she went on to the note. "Carter was on vacation during the third week in July. I've asked him to be our liaison with the FBI in a case they're working here, and he's scheduled to meet with agents at their office tomorrow. Should take most of the day. But you two be careful. Everything is still unsettled. Ray"

"Henry!"

He arrived, looked over her shoulder at the computer monitor, and his low whistle showed he was just as surprised as she. Finally he said, "I guess we know where that key went. Since Danielle's co-worker Kinley was with Carter at the party, we can safely assume they're still good friends this week. She's probably the one who dumped you, too."

"Call Ray."

"I will, but there isn't enough probable cause to do anything yet. All he can do is keep an eye on her if he chooses."

"Well, he'd better be keeping an eye on both of them. And why didn't Doug Boinevich say something about recognizing her when the three of us were at the museum? Wouldn't he have been at the party?"

"Not necessarily, but I will ask." He reached for the phone.

For her benefit he repeated Ray's answer to her question while the two men were still talking. "So he wasn't there," and then he said what she was thinking, "Good. I sure didn't want him to be part of this."

There was a silence while Carrie resisted the temptation to go pick up another phone and listen in. Then Henry said, "Uh-huh. Good idea... We will... I'll be in touch tomorrow." He put down the receiver.

"Good idea what?"

"He's going to ask Boinevich to visit the museum in the morning and have a chat with Kinley. He'll suggest she just might have seen that key. Maybe Danielle dropped it and Kinley innocently picked it up, not realizing who it belonged to—and so on. You know, the blather which sometimes gets we humans to open up in conversation and maybe tell more than we meant to. You used it with Danielle.

"Is Doug good at that?"

"I don't know if he has any special talent for it. Ordinarily investigating this kind of out and about stuff wouldn't be his job anyway, but Ray doesn't want to spread suspicions having anything to do with Carter around the department. He said Doug would understand. He's going to bring him in on all our discoveries now."

"You said 'We will.' We will what?"

"Watch our backsides."

"Should I be getting nervous about tomorrow's trip?"

"No need. Ray has seen to it Carter will stay in Kansas City all day."

"What about someone else who might be involved? Kinley, for example, or someone we don't know about.

Gordon Hawkins maybe?"

"They're watching Gordon and Danielle, and Ray will let us know if Kinley isn't at the museum as soon as Doug gets there. He has our cell phone numbers, and I'll keep mine clipped on my waistband, set to vibrate. Why don't you put yours in a pocket, just in case? If we don't hear from him, the path is clear. Ray agrees with us that it's all too probable Carter is deeply involved, but you're right, none of us can be sure of anything yet. Since Carter will be in Kansas City tomorrow, I think we can stay with our plan to visit Van Buren. Agree?"

"Yes. But my cell phone still doesn't work. It didn't like being dunked in the kids' boat ride pool."

"Oh, yeah, forgot. Doesn't matter. One will be enough."

There was no doubt about Jenni Lively's surprise when she saw the four of them coming through her front door the next morning. The shop looked the same as Carrie remembered, but the woman herself didn't. There was her twitchy nervousness; and her smile, when she finally managed it, was forced.

She ignored the silent Booths and said, "Did you bring the pendant?"

Carrie strolled to the counter while Shirley and Roger walked to the north end of the shop and began browsing, and Henry studied jewelry in a nearby display case.

"No, I didn't," Carrie said. "I meant it as a gift for a friend who lives in another state. I gave it to her several days ago."

"Actually," Henry said, coming to stand by Carrie, "as

I understand it from my wife, you bought that necklace at an estate sale. You purchased it in good faith for whatever the agreed-on price was. They have no right to ask for it back, nor do we need to return it. My wife paid your asking price."

For a minute, Carrie thought Jenni Lively was going to cry, but then she regained control, though pink blotches marked her complexion. "Well, I was...mistaken. I actually bought the necklace with a bunch of other jewelry from a dealer who came through here, and he's demanding its return. I know you don't have to sell it back to me, but...."

"Was the seller either of these men?" Henry laid photos of Graham Hawkins and Art Carter on the counter.

She was leaning forward to lay her finger on a photo when the first shot came, exploding a crystal vase next to where she stood. The clicks from scattering glass were barely audible in Carrie's ringing ears, but she heard the second shot clearly, and the shriek as Jenni Lively fell to the floor.

Instinctively she dropped as fast as Lively, and felt Henry at her side. Without any pause he pulled her along until both of them were behind the counter. The first thing Carrie noticed was blood. The second was the gun moving from under Henry's jacket and into his hand. *Oh God, oh dear God. Oh, no.*

Silence. Were the Booths safe? Had they seen this coming and escaped out the back?

More silence. Carrie looked at the woman lying next

to her on the cushioned floor mat. Where was that blood coming from? She followed the red back to its source, which seemed to be somewhere under Jenni Lively's blouse. *What should I do? God, help me.*

The answer was obvious. *Help her. And pray.*

A voice came from the silence. "The three of you are trapped. No way out."

"I'm armed, Carter."

"Really? With what? One of those vases? We all know you never carry a gun. Too much of a coward, a wimp, a quitter."

She felt Henry stir, felt his slight shudder. "Can you be sure?" he said.

"Ha. Prove you're armed, Mr. Coward King."

Carrie watched Henry's finger tighten on the trigger, then relax. He said, "Why waste bullets breaking crystal?"

The responding laugh was worse than any words Carter had said. Carrie's prayers moved into fast-forward.

Three footsteps, barely heard. Slow. Coming from an aisle against the south wall.

"I'll save my bullets until I can see you, Art."

Silence. Carrie took out her cell phone, looked at it. She'd put it in her pocket, just because. Would it work now? She pressed a button, heard a beep, stopped. What could Carter hear? If he thought she was using a phone, would he shoot to stop her? Henry was between her and the sound of Carter's voice.... She laid the phone on the floor mat.

Henry said, "What if customers come in?"

"There's no one out there now, and the excursion train doesn't arrive for another thirty minutes. We have time. Besides, when you've killed one person, why worry about a few more? Cops know how killers think."

Another chilling laugh.

"Graham Hawkins?"

"That stupid son-of-a... he was going to kill *me*. He even set his cousin up to take the blame if cops here got too close. I suppose he thought he was ready to carry on our very successful business without my help.

"We met at the river. He said he wanted to show me how clever he'd been, getting Chandler Wilcox to think he'd been able to salvage relics from a sunk steamboat. I'd told Hawkins he needed to upgrade the merchandise he was selling Wilcox, and his idea was Wilcox would be open to buying better stuff if he thought it had been found in a sunk Civil War boat and didn't suspect it was stolen. I guess the man had no problem with salvage from the bottom of the Arkansas, illegal or not."

"So you went out on the river together, and...?" Henry said.

"That morning Hawkins took Ms. Lively's skiff. We got in the boat and he rowed out to show me the smoke stack he'd rigged up in the center of the island, putting it together a section at a time. Said he'd already brought Wilcox to see his set-up, told him he'd found the *Sarah Anne*. Even showed him some old diving gear–which he'd never used, of course."

Carrie's cell phone vibrated against the mat. She

picked it up, listened to Ray speaking her name in exclamation points, telling her Art Carter hadn't showed up at the FBI meeting. She coughed into the phone, then put it back on the floor, hoping Ray could hear at least some of what was happening and call Burke.

Carter's voice droned on. "While he was rowing, his jacket gapped open and I saw he had a pistol. It looked like one of a working pair Kinley and I had lifted. No reason he would have just one unless he intended to use it on me. I figured out that's why we were going to the center of the island. A pop, a shove overboard, and I'd be gone. Noises from the factory loading docks above the river would hide any gun sound. He'd planned it well, I will say, but I got him first. Knifed the stupid blunderer when we got to the center of the island. A few quick shoves of the blade, then I held his face under water. Couldn't drop him out in the channel during daylight, so I pushed his body overboard behind the island. Used an oar to shove my bloody jacket down in the mud.

"When I took Lively's skiff back I saw a Kansas City car parked near her houseboat and figured it was Hawkins's. I didn't know about his cousin yet. Kinley found out about Gordon being in Van Buren from Danielle later. I searched the car to be sure there was nothing tying Hawkins to our business or to me, then tossed the keys from his pocket on Lively's deck with a note asking her to take care of my car until I got back. I signed it 'Graham Hawkins.'"

"I see," Henry said, sounding very calm.

Carrie supposed his phone had vibrated too, and he'd

chosen not to answer it. She'd been right then, Carter would act to stop phone contact. His voice droned on. Why was he telling them all this? Bragging? Showing how clever he was? She shuddered. It meant he thought their knowledge couldn't harm him. For a tiny minute she was tempted to stand and run for the door, shouting, "Don't hurt us!" She might make it. Carter would come out in the open, aim at her, and Henry would shoot him and... *NO!* She couldn't....

Carter was saying, "The only identifiable steamboat cargo Wilcox already had were buttons he bought at the Transport Museum in Kansas City, and those were reproductions. All the real nineteenth-century stock we were selling him came from small-town museums. Hawkins was taking him a bag of buttons–supposedly antique ones he'd found on the *Sarah Anne*–as more proof he really was getting salvage from a sunken boat. Wilcox thought most of the old stuff we'd sold him in the past came from estate sales and bankrupt shops."

"How about Kinley? I assume she helped with the museum thefts? Your pregnant wife?"

"A useful woman. Good at dumping nosy females into water." Another chuckle. "Yes, she played the pregnant wife, always wearing a wig and glasses. We rigged a place to put things we were removing right where the baby ought to be. See, superior intelligence. Graham played her husband a few times when I couldn't get away, but she said he wasn't much use, just paced the floor. He's well out of our way. And now you will be, too."

"Deputy Chief Duncan knows where we are today,

and who we were coming to see."

"Well, well. I wondered why I pulled that FBI assignment. But I had more important things to do. I needed to visit Ms. Lively. I wondered if she might be catching on to our operation since Graham left that emerald mixed in with the costume jewelry. Wilcox doesn't stock jewelry. He always consigned the stolen jewelry we sent him to Lively. A couple of our suppliers aren't good at telling fake from real, so they just grab everything. We have plenty of buyers for the good stuff, and this shop has proven a handy outlet for the junk.

"Of all the people she could have sold that stone to.... Well, it wasn't my mistake. Now there's going to be an armed robbery, and I get the pendant back with no more fuss. I suppose you brought it with you to honor her tearful request?"

"No. Ray Duncan has the pendant. He knows who stole it. He knows about you."

Silence. Carrie shifted her legs to ease cramped muscles, moving as slowly and quietly as she could. The silence continued. Where were Roger and Shirley? *God, keep them safe. Help me trust....*

Finally, "Okay King, show me your gun. Prove you have it. Hold it up." The voice came from their right. Was it closer? She hadn't heard any more footsteps.

"If you kill us, Duncan will know."

"Who cares? I've been ready to disappear for some time."

Carrie remained huddled on the floor, keeping an eye on Jenni Lively's slow breathing as she pressed a wad of tissue paper she'd found under the counter against the wound. There was less bleeding now. Surely that was a good sign. Carrie's thoughts returned to her prayers.

"Come on, where's your big bad gun, King?" The laugh was taunting, brutal.

Henry moved into a crouch. "If you don't believe I have a gun, walk out into the open and look at your picture on the counter. I put it there for Ms. Lively to identify. Ray sent it so I could see if Wilcox or Lively knew you."

"Useless move. I phoned her about the pendant. She hadn't seen me until today, and he never has. Now then, you might as well stand up. I need to get this over with, and make a quick trip home. I have to wipe out the problem of Gordon Hawkins too. He's become a nuisance, and is only alive because I didn't want more attention paid to the case while I was still around. After that, I'll finish a few other arrangements and be safely out of the country before anyone figures what's going on."

"Kinley?"

"Too bad, I'll miss her."

There was more silence while Carrie listened for footsteps. She looked up into her husband's face. *Determined, and so very strong. Henry King, do you know how much I love you? Do you know this gives me strength?*

"I'm coming, King. I've run out of time to play with you."

The gun, held in ready position, was right next to her

head. She could sense Henry's tension as she huddled between him and Jenni Lively–and now, she did hear footsteps.

Wired. They were wired....

When the enormous, explosive crash came, both their bodies jerked. She cried "No!" as Henry began to stand.

WILL WE DIE HERE?

When her attempts to hold him down failed, Carrie rose above the counter and stood beside Henry, looking at the wreckage. An entire shelf holding crystal and china had gone over, catching the bottom half of Art Carter's body under its weight. As if she were seeing the tableau in slow motion, she watched the upper part of that body lift a twisted face above the shattered china, heard him howl.

Roger, looking more surprised than frightened, stood in the aisle behind the shelf he had toppled.

Carter's howl turned into panted words, spoken after he'd laid his head back on the broken china and glass. "Finish... my story. Went back to check... saw him... musta been a boat wake... pushing him in." He stopped to breathe, then made a long, low humming sound before he spoke again. "Tried to shove him away... jogger came along... I left. Nothing to tie him to me... all done."

The head lifted again, showing a hideous grin. Beside it, Carter's hand held a gun pointing straight at her husband. "And now, Mr. Coward King, I fooled you."

Without conscious thought, Carrie shoved against Henry with all her strength, moving him far enough to escape the evil eye of the muzzle and filling that target space with her own body as the crack came. She felt the fabric of her jacket pull against her left arm. At the same instant a hot, tingling sensation zinged along her bra strap, and the jacket's shoulder pad exploded.

In the next second Henry's gun hand lifted. While

Carrie watched in awe he fired, sending the automatic in Art Carter's hand flying down the aisle.

"Oh, my... goodness," popped out of her mouth as Roger kicked through the wreckage to rest his foot against Carter's shoulders, and what looked like all the police officers in Van Buren, Arkansas burst through the front and back doors of the shop.

Tears and blood soaked into her jacket as Henry's body collided with hers and he grabbed her in a breath-crushing hug.

She heard Shirley say, "Sorry I couldn't get here earlier. Had to make it out the back door without that fella catching on so's I could call the police, but they'd already heard from a guy in Kansas City. At least I could tell them where you were. Any more casualties besides that lady, the killer under all those broken dishes, and you? You'd best let loose of her Henry so these guys can have a look at her shoulder."

He stood back and stared. "That monster *shot* you? Dear God, I'll..."

"Shhh," Carrie said, turning to Shirley. "Jenni Lively? She needs..."

"Those medical guys are tending to her. Now missy, hold still while I pull your jacket off. Careful, careful. Henry, make yourself useful and help unbutton her blouse."

"Little Love, Cara," was all Henry managed to say before his voice failed him.

Shirley, however, had plenty of voice. "Roger Booth," she said," you turn t'other way so Carrie won't be embarrassed." Carrie wondered how she was supposed to feel about the three male police officers, including Sgt. Burke, who were working to lift the heavy shelf Roger had shoved over. *Ah, well.*

"We're in your debt–again," she told Shirley as Henry laid his jacket over her good shoulder and across part of her chest, then took her hand in his.

"Shoot," Shirley said, "Adventures are just part of being friends with you folks. Good thing you moved to Blackberry Hollow right after our last-born left home. Life would have otherwise got mighty dull for Roger 'n me."

Carrie was wiping away tears and chuckling as the medical technician guided her into a chair and began inspecting the gouge across her shoulder. She winced a few times after that, but was back to chuckling by the time the woman finished mopping and prodding and said, "Doesn't require stitches, but you'll probably have a scar."

"Which she can be mighty proud of," Shirley said. "It's a reward for courage."

Shirley's usually right about a lot of things, Carrie thought as she said to Henry, "You'd better call Ray."

A CLEANSING EXPERIENCE

"I can tell you're feeling more settled now," Henry said, smiling at her across one of the plain plank tables in The Country Catfish Café.

They were enjoying exactly the same meal they'd shared there on their first date two years earlier, so the fact they were holding hands across the table seemed okay, no matter what nearby diners thought. Many people, Carrie decided, looking around, were startled when they saw grey-haired folks with... rather weathered faces, acting like love-struck newlyweds. *Which we are,* she thought, *one year today.*

She smiled all around and turned back to her own dear Henry, surprised and pleased that he'd noticed she was now at peace about events during the summer and fall. "Yes, I am settled. Knowing that Jenni Lively has recovered and is back in her shop helps, of course. Funny about her and Chandler Wilcox. I'm still not positive they didn't have a clue about sources for what Hawkins was selling them. What do you think?"

"I think we'll never know. There isn't enough evidence to make further investigation of them worth while."

"But, on the train, when the two men met? That's what made us suspicious at the beginning of all this. Had they planned on riding together?"

"I forgot to tell you about that. Burke said that Wilcox insists the meeting was a coincidence. Don't you think he's probably telling the truth? As I see it, the meeting was a negative for both of them. I'm sure Graham wasn't pleased about it because he didn't want anyone who could truly identify him to know he was in Van Buren. We know his reason for going there was to kill Art Carter. Of course he planned for Gordon to be a scapegoat if any trouble arose, but Wilcox would undoubtedly have noticed the difference between the two men if he got involved and the police showed him photos. So I guess Graham was as standoffish on the train as possible.

"In addition, maybe Wilcox was getting suspicious of the sunken boat tale by then, though he'll never admit he was aware of it. He wouldn't have wanted to be seen with Graham in case there was trouble in the future. Whatever the story is, I'm inclined to drop any suspicions when it comes to Jenni Lively and Chandler Wilcox. If there was criminal intent, it was slight."

"Okay, I agree. But what about Gordon and Danielle?"

"That's more difficult. I don't know how that case will come out. They have a good attorney, and there is no unbreakable proof they knew they were selling stolen goods. The fact Gordon closed out their bank accounts last August is suspicious, however."

"I've wondered if he wasn't planning to leave Danielle. Maybe he had grand plans about following in cousin Graham's footsteps somewhere else. If he had left, I don't think she'd have missed him much."

"Well, at least for a time, they're stuck with each other while their case goes to trial."

After a minute, Carrie said, "Y'know, after thinking things through, I'm sure everything that happened was how it was supposed to be, including those guys sitting in front of us on the train. It all unfolded logically toward resolution, one event after another. If we were the catalysts for some of that, well, that was meant to be, too. Of course Art Carter is partly paralyzed, but he brought it on himself. None of us can feel guilty, least of all Roger. I don't think he does... do you?"

"No. Both of us made it plain enough to Roger that we know he—and Shirley—saved at least three lives. Roger is too practical and too used to the ups and downs in nature and life to let Carter's condition bother him. Besides, Carter will get good care in prison. If he'd gone into the regular prison population he would have had to be separated anyway. Former cops don't last long among inmates in general.

"Ah."

"At least he confessed to us. Made it all easier."

"And there was that mud they found in our B&B suite. Riverbank guck still stuck in his shoes."

"Um-hm." He smiled. "Got enough hush puppies?"

She laughed. "You remember our first time here too well. I was sort of a pig about hush puppies. It really impressed me when you ordered me a second helping."

"Hush puppies—the way to a woman's heart?"

"You'd better believe it. A lot better than roses."

"At least to my very sensible wife!"

For a minute, they just smiled at each other, then Henry asked, "Is your shoulder really feeling okay?"

"It's fine. And Shirley was right about the scar. I'll think of it as a badge of courage."

"I... well, we... haven't talked about it, but I am very much aware that you saved me from Carter's gun. He'd aimed for my heart." He put a hand on his chest. "Which is just about shoulder height on you. You took the bullet he intended for me. Cara, a couple of inches farther over on your body and it could have...."

"But it didn't. That, too, was as it should be. Honestly, I never gave it a thought. I just shoved."

The look in his eyes said it all.

They continued to sit, holding hands across the table, moon-eyed and smiling.

RECIPES FROM CARRIE'S FRIENDS

Mama's Recipe for Saucy Hamburger (Courtesy, Rose Duncan)

Serves 4

1/2 stick butter
1 medium onion, chopped
1 lb lean hamburger
1/3 to ½ cup brown sugar
1 large can tomato sauce
1 teaspoon lemon juice
1 tablespoon Worcestershire sauce
1 tablespoon wet mustard
¼ cup ketchup

Melt butter in deep skillet or heavy kettle, add hamburger and onions and cook over medium heat, stirring until onions are tender (but not browned) and all the pink is gone from the hamburger.

Add remaining ingredients and simmer 30 minutes. Serve on toasted hamburger buns. (Put slices of cheese on the buns first if desired.)

Note: this recipe is easy to adapt or increase for large groups. If you want to serve the sauce over chicken or pork chops, melt the butter, stir in onion and cook until tender, then add the other ingredients (except hamburger) and simmer for 30 minutes. The mixture can be kept hot in a crockpot for buffet meals.

Dorothy's Chicken Casserole for Twelve

4 - 5 oz. cans chicken breast meat, drained
Enough prepared rice to make six adult servings
1 can cream of celery soup
1 can cream of chicken soup
1 cup diced celery
1 cup diced onion
2 medium-size jars pimentos, diced
4 cups frozen green beans, cooked
4 hard-boiled eggs, chopped coarsely

Salt and pepper to taste

Stir all together and place in greased 9 x 13 baking pan.
Bake at 350 degrees until hot and bubbling. If desired,
sprinkle with shredded cheese during last few minutes of
baking, or top with buttered breadcrumbs.

Note: This casserole can be assembled ahead of time,
stored in the refrigerator, and heated just before serving.

Chocolate Cake In a Mug (Henry's recipe)

Serves 1

4 tablespoons flour

4 tablespoons sugar

2 tablespoons cocoa

Tiny shake of salt

1 egg

2 tablespoons milk

1 tablespoon strong coffee

3 tablespoons oil

Small splash of vanilla extract

1 large microwave-safe coffee mug

Add dry ingredients to mug and mix well.

Add egg, mix well again.

Pour in milk, coffee, oil, and vanilla extract and stir until blended.

Put mug in microwave and cook for 3 minutes on High setting.

Don't be alarmed! Cake will rise over top of the mug.

Allow to cool a little; tip onto plate if desired, or eat directly from mug.

CPSIA information can be obtained at www.ICGtesting.com
Printed in the USA
LVOW06s2345240214

374948LV00001B/6/P